Callers For Dr. Morelle

Ernest Dudley

Table of Contents

Chapter One 5

Chapter Two 9

Chapter Three 15

Chapter Four 21

Chapter Five 25

Chapter Six 34

Chapter Seven 40

Chapter Eight 48

Chapter Nine 54

Chapter Ten 61

Chapter Eleven 66

Chapter Twelve 73

Chapter Thirteen 81

Chapter Fourteen 88

Chapter Fifteen 95

Chapter Sixteen 100

Chapter Seventeen 105

Chapter Eighteen 110

Chapter Nineteen 117

Chapter Twenty 124

Chapter Twenty-One 128

Chapter Twenty-Two 131

Chapter Twenty-Three 135

Chapter Twenty-Four 140

Chapter One

He had come in noiselessly, appearing in the doorway from the kitchen, before she realized anyone was there. She made a slim and young figure, graceful in her jeans and yellow sweater.

She faced him in the sitting-room of the cottage, and she felt desperately alone.

Outside the wind sighed gently round the eaves, rattled the windows now and again. She had been thinking that there was thunder in the air. It had been a warm day and the evening had brought up a stifling oppressiveness in the atmosphere, which even the slight wind failed to disperse.

She could hear a night-owl crying in the copse at the end of the little garden at the back. The copse would show up black against the sky, splashed with early stars.

Alarm was thrilling through her like an electric shock. She sensed the menace in his silent stare.

'What are you doing here?' she heard herself say. 'What do you want?'

He did not answer immediately.

He had not taken off his dark trilby hat, and it partly shaded his eyes. His eyes were small and round, dull and dead like little pieces of slate. They were always like that in his hollow-cheeked face, with its thin strip of moustache.

He was not much taller than she was, yet his shoulders were thick and heavily muscled. His arms tapered down to hands that were small in black silk gloves, almost feminine they looked.

Her uneasiness grew as she heard the ticking of the leather travelling-clock on the mantelpiece above the glowing fire become increasingly magnified.

It was an old cottage, low-ceilinged and black beamed.

The room was small, comfortably furnished, its curtains drawn across the low window, against the oncoming night. There were bowls of flowers on two small polished oak tables. One side of the fire-place held bookshelves, overflowing with a jostling miscellany of books. Glossy womens' magazines were scattered about. It was a little untidy, but it was warm and restful.

Or it had been until the man had come in.

At last he said:

'I just brought you a little present.'

His voice was cold, toneless. It went with the eyes in the shadowed face.

Puzzlement mingled with the fear in her lustrous brown eyes. The nostrils of her small, neat nose became pinched, her mouth paled underneath the lipstick.

'I don't want anything from you,' she said breathlessly, her heart thudding with fear. 'Leave me alone.'

His smile was only a slight twisting of the thin lips.

Some premonition of her dread fate struck home to her. Her innermost vitals seemed to coil within her. She knew now why he had sought her out the way he had done.

'No . . . no.' She was gasping, backing away as he began to move towards her, slowly, purposefully.

'I was sent to give you this,' he said. 'To give it to you nice and quiet, so that nobody will ever know.'

A hand came from his raincoat pocket. He held up a small object delicately between black silken finger and thumb. It gleamed in the light from the shaded electric lamp in the corner. She stared at it, in horrified fascination. It was a capsule. Sheer terror raced through her, sickening fright showed in her dilated eyes.

'What . . . is . . . that?' she found herself whispering.

The man smiled. That slow twisting of the thin lips beneath the moustache.

'Just cyanide,' he said softly. 'You won't know you've taken it, it's so quick. No trouble at all.'

She screamed, turning to run, to flee wildly from this deadly visitor. He leaped, striking like a snake. In the same movement he tucked the capsule inside his raincoat and in the breast-pocket of his jacket.

'Save your breath,' he snarled. 'There's nobody to hear you. There's just you and me.'

The small, steel-like hands held her, dragging her back.

Even then she could not believe she was going to die. She had suffered, she had thought once; not so long ago she'd wanted to die. So she had thought, during those long sleepless nights and hopeless dawns. But she was young.

She fought his merciless grip, beating at him with her fists, kicking, but it all made no impression on him. She did not even succeed in pushing his hat away from his eyes.

She was helpless against his dynamic strength. He flung her on to the divan, and held her down. One silk-gloved hand gripped her wrist, twisting her arm under her, so that she lay contorted to one side, her face turned up to him, her teeth bared in a grin of desperate agony.

Moaning, she still tried to fight him, writhing on the divan.

'Don't . . . don't,' she choked. 'For God's sake, don't do anything to me. I'll do what you want, what anyone wants.'

A quick movement and his hand that had gripped her wrist was suddenly pressing over her nostrils, turning her face up to him, while he still held her down on the divan. Her slim legs thrashed in the jeans, her mouth opened and she gulped for breath.

In that instant the other hand had slid deftly inside the raincoat. The capsule was in her mouth. She could feel it smooth and rounded on her tongue. The hand pressed over her nostrils shifted down over her mouth.

She could not breathe. Her eyes bulged with terror, suffocating, she was forced to swallow, and still he held her.

A violent spasm wracked her body. Her back arched, her face contorted. Mercilessly he held her there until she was still, an aroma of almonds came up to him as her mouth opened in a dreadful, twisted grin.

Now he stood back.

He took out a white handkerchief and wiped it across his moist forehead. He was breathing easily. The small, dull bits of slate that were his eyes had not altered their expression by a flicker. His shadowed glance went round the room, looking for any signs of a struggle. He righted a chair that had been pushed aside. He did not look again at the arched, twisted figure on the divan.

Nodding to himself in satisfaction he moved lightly to the door through which he had appeared. He closed the door after him, stepping out into the dark, tiny passage through to the kitchen.

He paused for a while, to accustom his eyes to the darkness as he made his way to the door at the back of the cottage.

Then he stiffened, every muscle tensed. He felt sure he had heard the creak of the front gate. Yes, those were footsteps on the path outside the front door. He heard a low, cheerful whistle. He cursed softly. Who was it who had to show up at this moment? Was it some friend of the dead girl?

Soft-footed, he continued across the kitchen, and in the darkness reached the back door, unlatching it quietly even as he heard the knocking on the front door. The knocking was repeated. He stood there, the door held open a little.

He shut the door quietly behind, letting the latch slip soundlessly into place. Then, a swift shadow he darted to the shelter of a bush in the dark garden. The knocking sounded yet again as he waited.

Would the newcomer go into the cottage, to find the girl so soon?

Tensely the man in the dark trilby stood there. He heard the whistling again, then the footsteps crunched away, he heard the front gate open and click shut.

He moved round the corner of the cottage and glimpsed a figure silhouetted against the lane, and pausing to tinker with the bicycle he wheeled from beside the gate. He watched the figure mount the bicycle and saw its wavering light as he pedalled away.

Relaxing, the man waited.

He was in no hurry, he wanted to make sure no one saw him quit the place. Nobody had seen him arrive, he was certain of that. No need to spoil things by bumping into some fool on his way out. He gave it some little time before he turned back and moved across the garden and was lost in the blackness of the copse.

Presently there came the sound of a car starting up in the road on the other side of the copse. A cigarette drooping from the corner of his mouth the man in the dark trilby peered along the beam of the car's headlights that probed the darkness.

As he let in the clutch he caught a flicker of lightning on the darkening horizon. He drove along the road until he came to the cross-roads and he took the turning for London.

He fancied he saw another lightning flicker to his left and he licked his lips nervously and stepped on the accelerator. If he made it snappy he might dodge the thunderstorm, get back before it broke.

He was terrified of thunderstorms, and the prospect of being caught in one in the car made him feel sick to his stomach.

Chapter Two

Phil Stone made Waterloo about ten minutes before the 6.45 was due to depart. Thankfully, he noted it was not very crowded as he walked down the platform, carrying his battered leather suitcase. He found no difficulty in securing a third-class smoking-compartment to himself.

It had been quite a day since he arrived at London Airport, and he did not wish to endure the discomfort of a crowded carriage. Hoping his solitude would remain undisturbed he lifted his suitcase on to the rack and sat back in a corner seat.

He took out a blackened briar pipe from his pocket and a well-worn pouch and filled the bowl automatically as idly he watched the bustle of the platform.

Above all, he wanted to be alone now, to surrender himself to thoughts of the girl he had journeyed half-way across the world to see.

His pipe drawing coolly, Phil settled himself stretching out his long legs, and automatically turned the pages of an evening paper he had bought at the bookstall. But his attention was not on the headlines or the news-stories.

Presently he heard the warning cries of porters, the shrill whistle of the guard, and his carriage began to slide noiselessly forward. An invisible hand slammed his door shut with a jerk of a handle.

Thank heavens he would be alone to Hatford, anyway. He would have to change there for Little Tiplow.

He sat still glancing unseeingly at his newspaper with his thoughts projected into the near future, when he would be with the one he wanted to see and be near to more than anything else in the world.

His face was deeply tanned, his hair bleached by the sun, there was a look of the sea and distances in his clear blue eyes. He was wearing a quiet double-breasted suit and a dark blue knitted tie. There was an essential simplicity and boyish frankness about Phil Stone's personality. It had remained unaffected by the arduous life he led, among the tough, astonishingly assorted men with whom he worked, in the long days and nights on rolling decks, or the blinding heat of oriental ports.

Lately his job had kept him in the Far East. Risen to ship's officer, there was the rewarding prospect of a master's ticket, if he decided to remain at sea.

This was his first home leave for over a year. A year it was since he had last seen Julie. He sighed, his thoughts went back to that visit to London, and the sudden, unexpected delight it had brought him.

During his voyages the colourful, hot and spice-laden glamour of the islands of the East had woven their spell about him. The rich green of those places of the South Pacific and the Coral Sea set like jewels against brilliant blue skies had held him with a powerful appeal. There was a deeply romantic side to his nature which, when with other people he would contrive to conceal beneath a pose of cynical experience.

But the appeal of the East had faded a little after he had met Julie Grayson. Smiling to himself, Phil put the newspaper to one side and as the train rushed onwards, he allowed his thoughts to dwell on the figure in the photograph which he took from his wallet. It had travelled with him across many tropical seas.

The photograph had been taken at a rehearsal. She was in practice-clothes, which showed her long, shapely legs and slim figure. She had been caught in a gay mood, her large brown eyes alight, her mouth was smiling.

Why, he wondered idly, had he fallen for the younger sister of the two? Thelma, five years older, beautiful in a more classic way, was tall and graceful, more serene than her volatile sister; the stronger character. Phil suspected she sometimes had a hard task to curb Julie's high spirits.

Both their parents were dead, and ever since they had left school, early in their teens they had worked as dancers in London shows and night-clubs. They enjoyed the life, with its ups and downs, its excitement and gaiety, and coping with its dull patches of being out-of-work, its depressing set-backs with the typical philosophy of people in show-business.

Neither of them fancied that they were particularly talented, they could dance well enough, they could sing enough to find their way through the trite chorus of a popular song; they both possessed personality and tremendous charm, they were quick-witted and amusing conversationalists. Nor were they hard or tough. That had surprised Phil most of all, their warm-heartedness, surprised him and attracted him.

He had met them at a cocktail-party given by a mutual friend, and he had been to see them in the show in which they were appearing at a big, popular night-spot.

There had followed that deliriously happy week in London, at the end of which he had become sure Julie, it was Julie he had fallen for from the moment he looked into her brown, amused eyes, was fond of him.

His leave over, he was off again, but he had written to her and she had written back and written again, and her letters had been warm and filled him with hope that they were meant for each other. Then had come the news that she had gone to work on her own in another night-club. From the hints she gave him in her letters, he did not like her new background, it did not seem to him that the move had been for the better; and maybe it had been his comments to this effect that had made her subsequent letters seem a little cooler and their arrival certainly less frequent.

When several hours earlier, Phil had reached London Airport, his contract ended, a few weeks' leave ahead before he signed a new one, he had gone to the tiny flat Thelma and Julie shared in Charlotte Street. Thelma had seemed delighted to see him, but there was no Julie. She had gone down to the little cottage in Hampshire, which had been left them by their parents and which, despite the ups-and-downs of their profession they had hung on to.

And so now he was on this train rushing through misty fields lying beneath the hazy sky of the September evening.

Phil glanced at his wrist-watch. Twenty minutes past seven. An hour-and-a-half and he would be at Hatford, and waiting impatiently for the local to take him to Little Tiplow.

Soon after he would see the lovely face that had filled his dreams all these long months, listen to her soft voice and amusing laugh. Would be glimpse in the lustrous depths of her dark-lashed eyes a promise he so longed to find waiting there? His heart beat more quickly at the thought.

It had been bad luck being delayed in London.

He might have caught a much earlier train, but there had been the fixing up of his rooms off Baker Street, recommended by a fellow-officer. The landlady had been out, and he'd had to go away and kill an hour or more before he had gone back and obtained the large bed-sitting room he wanted.

A call at the offices of the shipping-line he had served, a long wait there and then a long interview and then the visit to Charlotte Street. He hadn't rushed it. He had fully anticipated that Julie would be with Thelma at the flat. He had stored up the sight of her face as he arrived on the scene. He could not keep the mischievous smile from the corners of his mouth as he rang the bell.

But the smile had soon been wiped off his face. Julie had not answered the bell. It was Thelma, Julie wasn't there.

The recollection of his talk with Thelma brought a frown to his sunburned face. His eyes were unseeing as he gazed out at the flashing scene. Had there been a suspicion of something wrong? Had there been something a little edgy in Thelma's manner?

He thought of her long grey eyes, the dark hair, almost black with its marvellous sheen, her cool, controlled voice.

Was he wrong in sensing that her surprise and delight on seeing him there on the threshold had been tinged with doubt and anxiety? Her welcome had been warm and cordial enough, when she opened the door to him.

'Why, Phil. How wonderful to see you.'

He had gone in, looking for Julie.

'Don't be disappointed,' Thelma had said with a smile. 'She's not here.' And then she had hesitated, only for a second. 'She's . . . fine,' she had said in answer to his question. 'She's gone down to the cottage.'

Relaxing in the rather worn arm-chair, Phil looked around the room, very feminine, gay with flowers. From the kitchenette, as she heard the chair creak, Thelma had called out:

'Mind that chair, Phil. We bought it at the junk-shop round the corner. I don't know that it will stand up to hefty young sailor types.'

She came in presently with the tray, her grey eyes studying him, she looked cool in a blouse and neat black skirt.

'You should have let us know you were coming,' she said.

He grinned a little sheepishly. He was feeling pretty low over the anti-climax. It hadn't worked out a bit the way he had imagined it.

'It was all one of those last-minute rushes,' he said. 'The ship was paid off at Singapore, my company sold her to a concern out there, and then completely unexpectedly I found there was an air-passage vacant for me. The company wanted me in London to talk about promotion, so they were willing to pay my fare. I leapt at the chance, and thought —' he grinned again — 'I might give you a surprise.'

'It's a lovely surprise.'

'How are things? Isn't Julie still at this club?'

Had there been a hint of anxiety in her eyes, or had he been imagining it? 'Yes, she's still there. Only she — had had a few days off, they're beginning rehearsals for a new show. So she thought she'd pop down to the cottage.'

'She's down there by herself?'

'Just for a few days.'

Again he was remembering how he had been conscious of something evasive about her tone; an undercurrent of anxiety, was that what it had been? He had dismissed the idea then, he had put it down to his feeling of disappointment.

Then she had said: 'Why don't you go down?'

'Do you think there'd be a welcome on the mat?' Phil had said. 'I'll go now if you like.'

'Please do,' she had said. She had spoken quietly and he could have sworn that there was such urgency in her voice that he stared in surprise. But she had offered no explanation for her expression; and then his heart had begun to beat more quickly. Would Julie really want to see him, as much as Thelma seemed to be hinting?

'You seem to be on my side, anyway,' he had grinned at her.

'I'll wire her that you're coming. She can meet you with the local jalopy. The cottage isn't on the phone.'

'How do I get there?'

'Waterloo. Hatford's the junction down there, and you pick up the train for Little Tiplow. It always seems to me to be like a journey into the wilds of Darkest Africa, getting to Little Tiplow. But to a globe-trotter like you, it'll be nothing.'

She had found a railway time-table and he had fixed on the next best train.

'You can have my bedroom,' she'd said. 'Unless Julie insists on your having to stay at the local pub for fear of the scandal in the village, if it gets round that you both stayed the night under the same roof and no chaperone.' And she had laughed.

It was at the door of the flat just as he was going that she had told him she was at the same night-club as Julie. The Black Moth.

She would not have mentioned it to him, if he hadn't asked her how the show she was with was doing. She would not have volunteered the information, he had felt sure of that as he regarded her with a raised eyebrow.

'I made a move. Went over to this other joint.'

Her tone had been light.

'To keep an eye on the kid sister?'

His tone had been light, too. But at the back of his mind had been the hints Julie had dropped about the Black Moth in her letters to him.

'It's all right,' she had said to him, as if reading his thoughts. 'It isn't such a bad spot.'

He had felt then that there had not been very much conviction in her voice. He had thought she had sounded as if she was kidding herself. He must ask Julie all about the place, he had promised himself. And then he remembered that it was because of what he had asked her in his letters about the club, the anxious questioning, that had, he'd decided, brought the coolness in her letters to him, her letters which had reached him less often.

Then he heard Thelma saying:

'Phil, I'm so glad you've come.'

Then he had hurried away back to his room off Baker Street, quickly to pack a suitcase, whistling the song he had heard that time at the night-club when he'd first seen Julie in the show, his heart light at the prospect of seeing Julie soon. Yet that niggling shadow at the back of his mind growing more obtrusive, despite his attempts to brush it away.

It was Thelma's words to him: '*Phil, I'm so glad you've come,*' which were in his mind now as the train sped on to Hatford.

Chapter Three

Phil could not help contrasting Thelma's obvious pleasure at seeing him with her evasiveness about her sister. Oblivious of his cold pipe, he sat leaning back, staring out of the window.

A breeze was whipped in on him as the train sped through the oncoming dusk. He shivered slightly, recollecting that not long before he had stepped out of the aircraft in the heat of Karachi. The transition from the sweltering heat of the tropics to the cool of an English evening might be responsible for the sudden chill that passed over him.

He noticed that the haze on the passing fields had grown. In the sky a dark pall was looming up from the west. The sunset light was lurid, bronze in colour, and he knew that some dirty weather was blowing up. Maybe it was the impending storm which had all along been at the back of his mind's disquiet.

The growing darkness was caused not only by the approach of night, but by those black swollen clouds which were crowding the horizon. Hardly a good omen, he thought, with a rueful smile.

He raised the carriage window as a tang of smoke filled the compartment, beaten downwards in a long trailing plume by the heaviness of the atmosphere and sent swirling through the window. His thoughts kept in tune with the rhythmic monotony of the clacking wheels.

Presently he stirred, feeling the grinding pressure of the brakes, as the train slackened speed and swung into Hatford Station, its platform lights glinting in the dusk.

Phil knocked out his pipe, grabbed his suitcase and got out, glad to stretch his cramped limbs. A porter directed him, and he crossed the hollow-sounding bridge to another platform. The local for Little Tiplow was delayed, he learned, it was not expected for another half-hour. Impatiently Phil waited, pacing the platform. He wished that Julie could have met him at Hatford. He wished he had suggested it to Thelma, so that she could have put it in the telegram.

The local, a small fussy engine and two grimy coaches, wheezed into view and clattered pompously alongside the platform. For the last lap of

15

his journey Phil shared a carriage with a garrulous old man, smoking a foul-smelling black pipe.

'Fine old storm coming up,' the man said. 'Thought one was brewing. Been thundery all day.'

Phil nodded absently. He was in little mood for light conversation with strangers.

'Clear the air, though, that's one good thing,' the man went on. 'Rain'll come down in fair torrents, I shouldn't wonder,' he prophesied with conviction.

'I hope not,' Phil said with a slight smile.

'And last all night, I reckon.'

Phil did not answer. The rest of his replies were so monosyllabic that at last the old man was reduced to silence, except for a series of gurgling noises from his pipe. The engine puffed stertorously as it wound through a treeclad valley, dark and still.

Phil was thankful when at last the train panted into Little Tiplow. The station was merely a halt, with a short platform, and only a box of a booking-office and the glow from a signal-box further down the line. Phil got out, grabbing his suitcase and looked around. There was nobody in sight except a gangling porter who advanced out of the shadows and took his ticket.

The porter's answer to his query served to intensify his increasing gloominess of mind and uneasiness.

'No, I ain't see nobody. Been here all the time, and no one in no car's turned up.' His face was turned upon Phil blandly. 'They knew what train you'd be coming on, sir?'

'Yes,' Phil said, a trifle irritably. 'There aren't all that many trains, are there?' Had Julie got the telegram, he wondered, had Thelma sent it off in good time? 'A telegram was sent,' he said.

'Telegrams ain't very quick round here. The post-office don't always get a chance to send them out. If they're busy.'

Phil sighed heavily. 'I'd better just wait,' he said.

A quarter-of-an-hour passed.

To Phil, pacing the little platform disconsolately, the darkness pressing down, each minute seemed interminable. Every now and again the porter poked his head out of the booking-office door and made friendly inquiries.

A further fifteen minutes passed. When next the porter bobbed out with his parrot-like questions, Phil arrested his subsequent jack-in-the-box disappearance.

'I'm beginning to wonder whether my friend mightn't have had a breakdown,' he said.

'Maybe, sir,' the porter agreed with equanimity. 'It's dark enough and those winding lanes, might be in a ditch somewhere —'

'No need to be so damned cheerful about it,' Phil said. 'We'd better do something. How about phoning for a car, a taxi?'

The porter chuckled. 'You won't get anything like that tonight. The only one we got here clears off to Hatford arter the six o'clock comes in.'

Phil groaned. 'Then can't I telephone for one from Hatford?'

The other shook his head. 'It's like this. The Hatford drivers won't take no orders from here on account of trouble we've had with them not turning up as promised in the past. You might just as well try to get a special sent down from Waterloo, as get a hired car to-night.'

'All right,' Phil said. 'How far is Lilac Cottage from here?'

'Lilac Cottage?' The man pushed his cap on the back of his head. 'Let's see now.' He muttered to himself while Phil waited with growing impatience. 'I reckon it's about two miles. You turns down a little lane, first left — I think it's left — arter you gets to the cross-roads.'

'Good,' Phil said firmly. 'I'll walk.'

'Walk, sir? With this storm coming on? Why, look at it, dark as the inside of a black pig. And it's going to pour any minute.'

'I'm banking on it holding off for a bit,' Phil said. 'I'll risk it.'

Undoing his battered suitcase he took out a light plastic raincoat and put it on. With a grim glance at the sky he said good night to the porter and set off briskly.

What had the porter said? About two miles? As if it was any distance at all. Already he felt better now he had decided to walk. Kicking his heels on that comic little station had been a depressing business. It was good to have something definite to do.

With every step his spirits rose, the weight of foreboding seemed to be about to lift from his mind.

The storm burst upon him when he had covered about a mile.

In a matter of moments he was drenched, and cowering beneath the violence of the downpour. Lightning slashed across the sky and ripped apart the black, lowering clouds. Thunder crashed and rumbled; the rain driven by squall after squall stung his face with the sharpness of needles.

His raincoat was soon letting in the rain, which ran down the back of his neck, as buffeted by the storm, his trousers flapping, wet and uncomfortable around his ankles, his shoes squelching in the mud and puddles on the narrow road, he battled miserably forward.

No sense in stopping now. He might as well push on. Wryly he was reminded of those times when he had stood, hanging onto the ship's rail, battered and soaked by the fury of China Sea hurricanes. This was something like it, except that he was still on firm ground, and not on a reeling, creaking ship.

Barely able to make out the way, he staggered on. He found himself stumbling into a ditch. He stumbled against some thorny bushes, and cursed as he heard a rending sound, and felt the rain soaking through the tear in his raincoat.

Finding his way on to the road again, his shoes soggy in the mud, he pushed on. Suddenly his sense of humour took over, and he laughed aloud at himself. What a spectacle he must make, for a lover going to meet his girl. Rain-drenched, tattered raincoat flapping, splashed with mud to the knees.

'Phil Stone,' he roared at the storm, 'you're just about the biggest fool west of Suez.'

Tramping on, head down, he collided with something solid. He looked up. He had walked into the signpost which stood at the cross-roads. In the brief light of a flash from the sky he could not make out what the signpost said. But it didn't bother him. The gangling porter had said for him to keep on going past the cross-roads, and take the first on the left.

He could see only a few yards ahead. Suddenly he halted and he stood irresolute. Had that damned porter said left? He was sure he had. Somewhere along the road ahead of him he should turn left, that was it.

And then a watery, wavering light appeared in the darkness before him, drew nearer. It was a cyclist approaching along the road, he was coming from the direction in which Phil was about to head. Bent forward against the storm, the figure on the bicycle, Phil saw, was a man, hurrying as best he could.

Thankful for the sight of somebody who could reassure him that he was on the right way, Phil stepped out into the cyclist's path, waving his arms to attract his attention. The bent pedalling figure came on, apparently unaware of anyone in his path.

Phil let out a shout above the clamour of the storm. The cyclist jerked up his head. He seemed unable to understand that he was required to stop, he made no effort to slacken speed.

'Can you stop,' Phil yelled. 'I think I'm lost.'

This time the cyclist heard. He slowed down, and stopped alongside Phil, wobbling as his brakes slid on wet wheel-rims.

'Sorry, what did you say?' His voice was friendly. He didn't sound like one of the locals, it was a cultivated voice. 'Did you say you were lost?'

'I'm not sure,' Phil said. 'Sorry to trouble you, but I want Lilac Cottage. I'm a complete stranger, I'm afraid. I think this is the road, isn't it? That's what the porter at the station said.'

The cyclist, who wore a sou'-wester tied under his chin, and a glistening oilskin coat, produced a torch from out of his pocket. Phil noticed as it was switched on and was trained on his face, that the man had a leather bag hooked over the handlebars of his machine.

'Sorry, I'm blinding you,' the man said, and turned the torch, so that its reflection illuminated his own face; he had ruddy, weatherbeaten features, and keen eyes, wrinkled against the rain.

'Lilac Cottage?' he said. 'That's it, first turning on your left. About a hundred yards on.'

He jerked his head back indicating the direction from which he had come.

'Thanks so much,' Phil said.

'What a night, you must be soaked.'

'I'm all right, especially now I'm nearly there.'

'I'm in a hurry, I'm afraid.' The man's voice was resonant and warm. 'Just when my blasted car is in dock. Got a baby to help bring into the world, so I'll be shoving along.'

'Sorry to have stopped you, Doctor,' Phil said quickly. 'But I was afraid I might be off the right track.'

The other laughed good-humouredly, brushing the rain out of his eyes with one hand.

'You haven't got far to go now,' he said. 'You'll find it half-way down the lane. What a hell of a night.'

And as Phil again called out his thanks, the man pushed off and pedalled into the darkness.

Phil turned to stare back at the dark figure and the wobbling red rear-light until it vanished, then he went over the cross-roads, peering ahead for the turning on the left.

As he came to the lane, it suddenly struck him that the wind had dropped, the rain had almost ceased. The thunder was growling away in the distance. He saw lightning rimming the clouds on the horizon with an electric blue shimmer. The storm had blown itself out as quickly as it had begun.

He stood for a moment listening to the drip-drip from the branches of a nearby tree. Then he turned into the lane, with a grin of anticipation and a quickening step.

Chapter Four

Lilac cottage stood white and low-built back from the lane and as he opened the gate and went up the little path, his soaked shoes making no sound, Phil suddenly glimpsed what appeared to be an appropriate lilac tree in a corner of the front patch of garden.

The cottage was distempered white with beams picked out in black. It was one-storeyed, its slate roof glistening in the gloom. A porch faced him, on either side of which was a window.

The thrill of expectation that had uplifted him ran higher now. At last, he was so very near to his heart's desire.

He caught an edge of light round the curtained window on the left of the porch as he put down his suitcase and reached for the brass knocker. His rat-tat echoed beyond the front door and he pictured Julie's face as she heard his knock. He hoped she would not be startled too much. She wouldn't be used to visitors out of the night, he imagined. That was assuming she hadn't received Thelma's telegram, and it remained to be seen what had happened about that. He would not have to wait long to know for sure, he told himself.

There was no sound of movement within. Only the sigh of the wind round the cottage and the sound of rain dripping from the trees nearby. A few moments passed as he stood there, staring at the door, chilled and damp round the back of his neck. He could feel the water that filled his shoes seeping out onto the stones beneath them. His trouser turn-ups were sticking to his ankles.

Still no sign of Julie having heard his knock. Far away came the faint sound of a train, the little sound seemed to intensify the silence around him.

He banged the brass knocker again, more loudly this time. A squall of wind swirled into the porch, and a cold rivulet of water ran down his back inside his bedraggled collar. He wondered if Julie had the radio on and had not heard him for that reason, but he could hear nothing within.

His teeth chattering a little reminded him that he had become used to the tropical weather, where even the rain was warm. He banged on the door once more. Much louder this time. What an anti-climax to the wearisome journey this was.

He recalled what the porter had said about the telegram. If in fact it hadn't been delivered for some reason, though he hadn't taken the man's observations about the local post-office seriously at the time, but if Julie wasn't expecting him, she might have gone out.

He glanced out of the porch at the window with the edge of light round the curtains. Why was the light on? He supposed she could have gone out and forgotten it. Or left it on so that anyone passing, a tramp or someone like that, would not guess that the place was unoccupied. A dozen reasons went through his mind which would explain the silence that had greeted his arrival.

He realized he ought to have given it more thought. He had been so buoyed up by wishful thinking, he had failed to foresee a dozen eventualities which could easily have prevented Julie from expecting him. It would explain the non-arrival of any hired car to meet him. It would explain why he was standing here, soaked to the skin and bedraggled, wretched and his spirits rapidly sinking to a low ebb.

Or even if the damned telegram had reached her, she may have had previous commitments which had prevented her from meeting him at the station or being at the cottage. He looked about him for signs of a note which she might have written him and left by the door. But there was nothing.

His mind harrowed with conjecture he tried to decide what he should do. Hadn't Thelma said something about a village pub? He'd better make tracks for that, and get out of his wet clothes and put a warm drink and some food inside him. And yet he hated the idea of going away. Julie might turn up at any minute for all he knew.

He gripped the door-handle and turned it. The door did not open. It was locked. The thought that had occurred to him of waiting for her in the cottage died.

Still refusing to give up hope, not wanting to go away, he stepped out of the porch and leaving his suitcase where it was, made his way round to the back.

He made out the black silhouette of the small copse at the end of the garden. The night sky appeared lighter now, stars were beginning to pierce the darkness over-head. Only the distant mutter of thunder, that was all that was left of that sudden, short-lived storm. Stumbling against a brimming-over water-butt, he came to the back door.

There was still silence inside the cottage. He saw no light anywhere.

A feeling of desperation swept over him. His nerves were edgy with fatigue and hunger, his spirits dejected by the sequence of irritating incidents that seemed to have heaped themselves one after another upon him from the moment he had stepped off the train at Little Tiplow. How much longer would he have to hang around in his soaked clothes and sopping shoes?

On an impulse he tried the back door latch. To his astonishment, it yielded to his first touch. The door opened.

What had happened, he decided was that Julie had gone out, locking the front door behind her, forgetting that the back door was unlocked. It was not unlike her to do something like that.

For a moment he hesitated, then he stepped inside. He found his lighter and snapped it alight.

The flickering yellow flame showed him that he was in a small kitchen. He looked around for a light-switch. He saw it beside another door which was open onto a short passage, beyond which, to his right, lay the front room whose light he had seen behind the curtains. There was silence, except for the loud ticking of the kitchen clock on the wall. He gave a little start as he heard a clatter in the front room.

'It's me,' he called out. 'Phil. Anybody at home? Julie, you there?'

His voice seemed to linger in the eerie stillness, then die away.

And then quite suddenly an inexplicable dread surged through him to the exclusion of every other emotion. His heart thudded heavily; the back of his throat was dry, and a chilling sensation beginning underneath his scalp, moved slowly down his spine. The abysmal dread was gnawing at his very soul, and as he stood there hesitating he could not shake it off.

'Hell's bells,' he said aloud, and shook his head as if to clear the mist of apprehension that had engulfed him.

Before him showed the light streaming from the lighted room. A staircase was on his right, and he glanced up into the darkness. On his left, opposite the staircase was a large cupboard door. It was open an inch or so.

He went forward slowly, indecisively.

Ahead of him at the end of the dim passage, but caught in the edge of light which came from the room on the right, he saw something which lay on the door-mat. He stood outside the room eyeing it miserably, and then he bent down and picked up the telegram.

So it had been delivered all right. But not in time to catch her before she went out.

He turned towards the sitting-room, he could see the red flicker of a fire, its embers were dying down. He smelled the tang of smoke, and then saw that a piece of charred log had fallen out onto the hearth.

That must have been the clatter which he had heard a few minutes before.

So Julie must have been at home earlier that evening. The fire could only mean that. And that telegram had arrived too late.

Risky of her, he thought, frowning a little to himself, leaving the fire burning like that, without any guard to prevent embers from falling and perhaps reaching the rug which lay only a foot or two from the fire-place. It was that in his mind which prompted him to step into the room.

He went over and picked up the piece of log, its aromatic tang stronger in his nostrils. He put it back on the fire, and sparks flew up. He straightened himself and turned to look round the warm, comfortable room.

That was when he saw the figure sprawled on the divan, her head thrown back, the eyes staring open, the mouth drawn over clenched teeth, the face twisted in agony.

Chapter Five

Phil Stone sat, his gaze fixed on the Coroner's chair which was on a dais at one end of the room in the town hall which served as the Coroner's Court. The light-painted walls of the room were plain and drab-looking, the curtains which were drawn back looked nondescript and faded, only the September morning sunlight which streamed through the tall windows brought a look of cheerfulness to the surroundings.

Thelma Grayson sat beside him, quiet and calm, but her beautiful features were pale and drawn, her eyes shadowed with grief.

The room was fairly full. There were rustlings and whisperings, the scrape of a chair. The jury, composed of eleven Hatford residents, sat in their places already; local tradesmen and business men, clerks and artisans, called from their everyday occupations to listen to the story of Julie Grayson's death and return their verdict upon how that death had come about.

It awaited only the arrival of the Coroner himself for the proceedings to start.

And while the Court waited, Phil's mind was going over again for the thousandth time that dreadful night at Lilac Cottage.

How he had managed to pull himself together after the first shock of seeing that frightful sight on the divan, how he had made vain efforts to revive Julie, trying to bring back warmth and movement in the stiffening, cooling, contorted body. Realizing how hopeless his efforts were, he had looked round for a telephone. Remembering there wasn't one, he had rushed out of the cottage to fetch help, even although he knew it was too late.

He remembered finding his way along the dark roads to the village, and the Half Moon Inn where he had phoned the local policeman, who had gone with him to Lilac Cottage. That was after the doctor had been sent for, and Phil had phoned Thelma.

Then there had been the police-inspector and his sergeant from Hatford. The inspector had questioned him, while the sergeant had roamed round the cottage, the first shock beginning to recede and a cold, empty feeling taking its place. Then the ambulance from Hatford to take Julie's body to the mortuary in the town.

It was Phil who had drawn attention to the telegram, and explained how it came to be sent. Later, he learned that the postman's son had been interviewed, and had given his explanation about the telegram being delivered when he had a free moment.

'Lilac Cottage was in darkness,' he told the police. 'I couldn't make anyone hear, so I thought they was out. Just shoved the telegram through the letter-box, and biked home quick. There was a storm coming on.'

That fixed the time. Julie must already have been dead when Thelma's telegram arrived. Would it have saved her, if she had read it? Over and over again Phil had asked himself that agonized question.

He glanced at Thelma now, as she sat, composed and pale, only her shadowed eyes showing the torment she suffered.

She had not been at the Charlotte Street flat when he had telephoned. He had forgotten about that at the time, remembering it only when he heard the no reply burr-burr. And so he had got on to the Black Moth, and while he waited for her to come to the phone, he could hear the dance-music behind her, and he had tried to work out words and phrases, a way in which he could soften the shock of what he was going to tell her.

'Thelma,' he had said to her when he had heard her voice, the dance-music still there incongruously behind her, 'I'm afraid you must brace yourself for — for a shock'

'What's wrong, Phil? Julie ill?'

Her words overlapped his as he was saying: 'It's bad news, I'm afraid. It's —'

'Bad news?' It seemed to him that there had been no alarm in her voice. 'Phil, you haven't had a row?'

Why should she have said that? It had gone through his mind at the time. Why should she have thought that he and Julie had quarrelled? But he had been too preoccupied to find the words to tell her that Julie was dead. Somehow he got the words out. The dance-music was still there behind her.

'I must come down,' she had said. 'I'll come down right away.'

It was as if she was speaking automatically, as if the real truth of what had happened had not sunk in.

'But — how?'

'I'll get a hired car.'

She had arrived at Lilac Cottage two hours later, in a black saloon hired car. Phil was awaiting her. Julie's body had been taken away. Phil had accompanied her to Hatford police-station, and then to the mortuary, to identify her sister. She was the dead girl's only living relative.

And Phil was recollecting how in the police-car she had said to him, her voice low and suppressed: 'I must see her. I want to remember.'

The strange phrase had stuck in Phil's mind ever since. He recalled her evasiveness when he had arrived unexpectedly at the flat at Charlotte Street.

He had remembered wondering at the time why Julie had gone down to Lilac Cottage alone, and that Thelma's explanation that she had taken a week's holiday while the new show was being rehearsed at the Black Moth had sounded vaguely unconvincing even to Phil, whose knowledge of the workings of show-business was nil.

'Why should she have done it?' he had asked her.

And she had looked at him mutely, dry-eyed, frighteningly self-possessed. It was after they had come from the mortuary, and he had stood with her and the police-officer silently staring down at Julie as she lay in the cold, hygienic surroundings, Thelma had formally identified her.

'What could she have been so unhappy about?' he'd said.

'Phil,' was all she had said, 'if only that telegram had arrived in time.'

That telegram that might have saved her life. If Julie had known that he was on his way, she might not have been lying there. But it didn't explain why she had killed herself, it didn't explain Thelma's evasive reply to his question. Julie, she'd said, had not been happy lately.

The rustle of the Court fell away into silence, broken by the loud tones of the policeman who acted as Coroner's Officer.

'The Court will rise.'

Phil and Thelma, with the jury, the medical and police witnesses, reporters from the local papers, and the scattering of people in the public seats rose as the Coroner entered through a doorway behind his chair.

A brisk little man, he nodded as he sat down. He was grey-haired, a sallow fine-lined lawyer's face, serious now as he looked round the court through gold-rimmed pince-nez.

'The Court is open.'

The Coroner paused for a few moments, then he turned to the jury, who sat somewhat self-consciously on his right. The police-officer read out the eleven names. When that was over the Coroner cleared his throat.

'We are called here to-day to inquire into the circumstances surrounding the death of Miss Julie Grayson, and your duty will be to inquire how, when and where the deceased came by her death. All relevant witnesses will be called. You will hear all the evidence, and you will be asked to give your verdict as representatives of the public at this inquest. I will give you all the guidance you need. Do not hesitate to ask any question if there is a point on which any of you is not satisfied. Is that understood?'

A portly, red-faced man who looked like a butcher, and who had been elected foreman of the jury by the others, said:

'Yes, sir.'

'Then we may proceed.' The Coroner took off his pince-nez, put them on again and glanced at the sheaf of papers on the baize-covered table before him, and spoke to the officer.

'Call the first witness.'

The policeman from Little Tiplow was the first into the witness-box on the Coroner's left and took up the Bible.

'I swear by Almighty God that the evidence I shall give shall be the truth, the whole truth and nothing but the truth.'

The truth, Phil thought bitterly, the truth was that the girl he loved had been found racked and tormented, dead, and not all the paraphernalia in the wide world could bring her back to life again.

'You are the police-officer in charge at Little Tiplow?' the Coroner asked him.

'Yes, sir.'

'Please proceed.'

The round-faced policeman cleared his throat and glanced at his notebook.

'At approximately 9.55 p.m. on September 6th last, I was called from the police-station to the Half Moon Inn, Little Tiplow. There I met Mr. Phil Stone, who informed me he had found a young woman dead at Lilac Cottage. He had just come from the cottage to get help. After sending someone for Dr. Walsh, who was out on a confinement, I proceeded to Lilac Cottage with Mr. Stone. I found the front door locked, but gained entrance through the kitchen door, which was on the latch. The lights were on in the kitchen and in the sitting-room, where I found the deceased lying on a divan covered by a raincoat.'

Phil heard the slight gasp of an indrawn breath beside him and felt Thelma's arm, quivering and tense against his. His hand went to hers, comfortingly. Her hand was as cold as ice beneath his. He was seeing again the scene in the sitting-room before he went to the Half Moon Inn.

He could recall trying to force his numbed brain to take control of his thoughts and actions once more. He had glanced around the sitting-room, looking for a glass or phial which must have contained the poison. He searched the floor by the divan. There was nothing. How had she taken the deadly poison? Into his mind had flashed stories he had heard of people on the run, escaped criminals who had carried poison capsules on them, sometimes in their mouths, so that they could cheat their pursuers at the last moment. Something like that must have come into Julie's hands.

Like a man in a dream he had taken off his raincoat and placed it tenderly over her. He wanted to remember her as she had been, as she was in the photograph in his pocket, not as she was now, her face contorted in a grin of agony.

He had gone out through the back door, pausing to pick up his suitcase from the porch then putting it down again, and hurrying down the lane, in what he took to be the direction of the village.

The policeman in the witness-box was continuing in stilted official phrases: 'I ascertained that the deceased was dead. I questioned Mr. Stone further as to how he came to discover the deceased, and during the course of these questions Dr. Walsh arrived. I therefore left the doctor and Mr. Stone at the cottage, and proceeded to the police-station to telephone the police-station at Hatford, then I returned to Lilac Cottage, where Dr. Walsh and Mr. Stone were waiting for me.'

'When you first examined the deceased did you form any opinion of the cause of her death?'

'Yes, sir,' the policeman said. 'I was of the opinion that she had taken poison.'

'No doubt you examined the room. Was there any indication of how the deceased had administered the poison to herself?'

'No, sir.'

'No glass, no bottle, no phial, which had contained it?'

'I examined the divan and the floor around it, I found nothing of the sort, or any sign that any such object had fallen there.'

'Thank you, you have given the Court a very clear idea of the situation as you found it. Please remain in case I should have any further questions to ask you. Call the next witness.'

'Call Dr. Leonard Walsh.'

Phil remembered the first time he had seen Dr. Walsh battling his way through the storm on his bicycle, that night.

'The Court has been told that you were called to Lilac Cottage, Dr. Walsh,' the Coroner said. 'Will you tell us what conclusions you came to as a result of your examination of the deceased?'

'I examined Miss Grayson,' Dr. Walsh said. 'She had been dead for about an hour, I should say. The cause of death was immediately obvious to me. She had been poisoned by a dose of cyanide. There were the characteristic symptoms — extreme dilation of the eyes, the teeth clenched, the rigid contortion of the body and the clenched hands, blueness of the face and lips, and bitter odour of almonds about the mouth.' He paused, shrugging his shoulders. 'There was nothing I could do.'

'Death would have ensued very quickly?'

'Immediately. It was obviously a large dose, and failure of the heart and respiration would have resulted in a matter of seconds, preceded by convulsions.'

'You knew the deceased?'

'Not exactly. I knew she and her sister lived at Lilac Cottage. I had seen them both in the village. But she never came to me for treatment at any time.'

'Can you give us any idea how the poison was taken?'

'Apart from the fact that it was taken through the mouth, no sir.'

'I mean, was it swallowed from a glass, or phial?'

'Since there were no signs of a glass or anything which could have held the poison, I can only assume it was swallowed in a capsule or something of that kind.'

The police-pathologist, Dr. Edwards, was next in the witness-box, a small, mild-mannered man.

'You carried out a post-mortem on the body of the deceased, Dr. Edwards?'

'That is so,' Dr. Edwards said. He spoke quickly in a brisk voice, with a ring of authority in it. 'My examination,' he went on, 'confirmed Dr. Walsh's earlier diagnosis. The primary cause of death was heart-failure, caused by the intake of an exceptionally large dose of cyanide. About twenty grains I should say, or its equivalent. The deceased was physically healthy, with no sign of organic disease.' He glanced towards Phil and Thelma. 'I'm sure you won't require me to go into all the details of the examination I conducted, they are not relevant, sir, I assure you.'

The Coroner nodded, as he glanced at Thelma. 'Quite,' he said. 'But we should like some explanation of the manner in which the poison was administered.'

'There were some traces of some gelatinous substance still in the mouth. I gather from the police evidence that no receptacle was discovered at the scene, so I am prepared to state with reasonable certainty that the poison was taken in some sort of capsule. As has been suggested by Dr. Walsh.'

The Coroner considered this for a moment. 'In other words it was all ready for use, in this concentrated form?'

'Yes, sir.'

'A person having such a capsule in his or her possession would presumably know something of the possible effect?'

The man in the witness-box hesitated momentarily. 'Almost certainly I would imagine. But knowing its effects, I should have thought there would have been some hesitation about using it.'

'I see, Dr. Edwards,' the Coroner said quietly. 'It is not a pleasant way of taking life.' He removed his pince-nez, blinked down at the papers on the table, then replaced his pince-nez once more. Glancing at the jury, his eyes then went round the court, before coming to rest on Dr. Edwards. 'I am correct, am I not,' he said, 'in presuming it would be difficult for any ordinary member of the public to secure any quantity of this poison?'

'You are quite right, sir.'

'It is not for me to say how the deceased came to possess the poison,' the Coroner said, 'but there are definite regulations as to the sale of any poisonous substance, made under the Dangerous Drugs Act of 1951.' His voice trailed off while he stared over his pince-nez at a reporter, who was busy scribbling, then turned back to the witness. 'Your view, Dr. Edwards, is that the deceased could have taken the poison herself in the form you suggested?'

'Yes,' the doctor said with a nod. 'With the reservations I have made as to its effects, which almost certainly would have been known to the deceased.'

'Quite, quite,' the Coroner said quickly. 'That leads us into other aspects of this sad case, such as the state of the mind, which we still hope to investigate.'

'One point,' Dr. Edwards said, 'is that during my examination I noticed some slight bruising round the nostrils and jaw. I mention it in passing, though I attach no importance to it.'

'Can you account for those bruises?' the Coroner asked.

'It seemed to me that a person taking this poison in such a form, might experience some revulsion at the last moment before swallowing it. The bruises would be consistent with holding the mouth closed firmly to aid the act of swallowing.'

The Coroner nodded understandingly, then, after rustling his papers for a few seconds, he said: 'Thank you, Dr. Edwards.'

The police-inspector was next in the witness-box. A tall man, his grey hair cropped short. He described how, on receiving the call from the policeman he had driven to Little Tiplow with a detective-sergeant. They had searched the room in which the deceased lay, and had continued their search through the cottage.

'There was no trace of any other person having been present, apart from Mr. Stone?'

'No, sir,' the inspector said. 'According to our investigations Miss Grayson had been alone before Mr. Stone arrived. I arranged for the body to be taken to the mortuary, having heard Dr. Walsh's opinion, and informed your officer.'

'Is there any other point about your investigation of the cottage which you wish to bring to the Court's attention?'

'Only the matter of the telegram, sir. Mr. Stone drew my attention to it. It had arrived that evening. It had not been opened, so I opened it. I understood from Mr. Stone that he had found it when he first entered the cottage. I questioned the postmaster at Little Tiplow post-office,' the inspector continued. 'The telegram was received over the telephone at 5.45 p.m. It was delivered by the postmaster's son at Lilac Cottage at approximately 7.50. The postmaster's son explained to me that he was delayed by a puncture to the tyre of his bicycle, and that when he got to Lilac Cottage, which is about a mile-and-a-half from the village, no one answered his knock. He thereupon pushed the telegram through the letter-box and went off.'

'I have the telegram here,' the Coroner said, as he took the buff form from among his papers. 'It is addressed to Miss Julie Grayson. 'Phil back unexpectedly,' he read. 'On his way down to see you this evening. Stop. Meet him station. Stop. All my love darling Thelma.' He glanced at the jury. 'The deceased, of course, had not read this telegram,' he said. 'It arrived too late. Perhaps it is unfortunate that it did so.' He eyed the telegram for a moment over his pince-nez. Then:

'Call Mr. Phil Stone.'

Chapter Six

The Coroner led Phil through his story up till the time of his discovery of Julie lying there dead at Lilac Cottage. The Coroner had asked him only a few questions, but now he said:

'Let me put it this way, Mr. Stone, had anything happened in your relationship that might cause Miss Grayson to be unhappy?'

'None that I know of, sir' Phil said.

'You were engaged to be married?'

'No. I was in love with her, and intended to ask her to marry me.'

The Coroner nodded sympathetically. 'Can you answer this question? Can you give me any reason, or do you know of any possible reason, why Miss Grayson should have taken her own life?'

'I just can't understand it, sir.'

The Coroner paused for a moment, a frown appearing above the glint of his pince-nez. 'The Court has heard something of what must have happened on that tragic night, the medical and police evidence has accounted for much,' he said. 'Now, when you finally reached Lilac Cottage, what did you do?'

Phil told of his wretched, bedraggled state, as he fought his way through the storm, of his encounter with Dr. Walsh; of his arrival at Lilac Cottage, the light shining in the sitting-room window. He told of his disappointment at receiving no answer to his knock, and his trying the back door. He told of his discovery of the unopened telegram. 'I went into the sitting-room,' he said, 'and then I found her.'

'You found the room exactly as described by the police?'

'Exactly,' Phil said.

'There is just one other question, did you know any friends of Miss Grayson?'

'No, sir. I just knew she worked at this night-club in London, and I learned later that her sister was at the same club with her.'

And then Phil returned to his place. Now the Coroner looked directly at Thelma.

'Miss Grayson, needless to say, you have my deep sympathy and I do not want to distress you more than you have been distressed already. But I should like you to give evidence, if you will come into the witness-box.'

Phil watched her as she took the oath, her slender fingers twisting a wispy handkerchief. Otherwise she appeared calm and composed. She wore a severely-cut black suit and a small black hat. She wore little make-up. Phil heard someone behind him whispering. Someone ghoulishly discussing the night-club girl whose sister had died violently and suddenly? he wondered.

The Coroner came quickly to the question.

'Tell me, Miss Grayson, was there any known reason why your sister should have been unhappy? Anything connected with her work for instance?'

Phil watched Thelma as she hesitated. 'She was normally gay and friendly,' she said.

'You have not answered my question.'

Thelma was silent for a few moments. 'She hadn't been very happy lately.'

'Yes?' The Coroner prompted her gently.

There was a long pause, and Phil clasped his hands together. Thelma had turned to look at him, and he saw that there was an unfathomable expression in her eyes. Again he thought he observed the deliberate evasion of something in Julie's life which Thelma did not wish him to know.

The Coroner sighed, as if to say he had arrived at the tricky stage in the proceedings. He would have to exercise all his tact and patience, all his sympathy and understanding. This was the dead girl's sister. She probably knew the answer to everything. 'No doubt,' he said, striking out on a new tack, 'your sister made a number of friends in the course of her work at this night-club?'

'Yes.'

'We have learned that your sister enjoyed her work, that she had no financial worries, but you have hinted that of late she had not been quite so . . . happy. Yet you have not told us why. I do not wish to distress you unduly. But this Court has to decide whether your sister took her life, and if so what caused her to do so. Please answer my questions, as best you can, Miss Grayson. Had your sister formed some romantic attachment which might have caused her unhappiness?'

There was a moment of suspended activity in the plain drab room with the morning sun, now paler, as if the day had grown chill; every eye fixed on Thelma Grayson. Phil thought he caught a quick glance from her from the corner of her eye in his direction.

'If I must answer, I will do so.' Her voice was almost inaudible. 'I was worried because she had fallen in love — she had become infatuated with a certain man.'

Phil felt a pulse beating over his right eye as he heard the hesitant words, and his jaw tightened.

'You do not mean Mr. Stone?'

'No, sir.'

'May we know who this man was?'

'He owns the Black Moth,' Thelma said quietly.

For a few moments the Coroner regarded her, then with a flickering look at his papers, he said: 'Thank you, Miss Grayson.' Now there was a brisk, satisfied inflexion in his tone.

Thelma looked at him from the witness-box in surprise. Phil saw the sheer relief sweeping over her face, then her face clouded as she went towards Phil to take her seat again beside him. Phil smiled crookedly at her to reassure her.

'I'm sorry, Phil,' she whispered as she sat down.

He pressed her hand understandingly, reassuring her again.

The Coroner was looking at the jury. 'I formed the opinion that some explanation of this unhappy girl's death might be found at her place of employment,' he said. 'Accordingly I suggested that this might be the case to the police,' he turned to the police-inspector. 'Has anything been done about that?'

'Yes, sir. On your advice I telephoned the West End Central Police Station in London. An officer from there went to interview Mr. Ray Mercury, the owner of the night-club in question. Mr. Mercury said he would be here to give evidence.'

Phil heard Thelma gasp beside him, give a little moan.

'No, no.'

'Where is Mr. Mercury? Is he here to give his assistance?'

The police-officer glanced across to the door.

'I was told he was on his way, sir, he should be —'

There was a sudden bustle outside the opening of the door, and everybody turned as a slim man of middle height, dark-haired, his face curiously softly moulded and yet with a ruthlessness in it, came in. He was dressed in a well-cut dove-grey suit and wore foreign-style shoes, and there was about him an air of opulence and impeccable grooming.

'This is Mr. Mercury now, sir,' the inspector said.

The newcomer was murmuring apologetically. Phil noted that his voice was as soft as his expression, and his whole personality was withdrawn and secret. It was a fault with his car, he explained to the Coroner, which had accounted for his delay. He did not seem to notice anyone around him, his entire attention seemed to be concentrated on the Coroner.

Phil threw an oblique glance at Thelma, as Mercury made his way into the witness-box. He was shocked at her expression as she leaned forward. Mercury had not even glanced in her direction, but her gaze was fixed on him. Her pale beautiful face was charged with hatred and her long, grey eyes glittered feverishly.

Phil turned to look at the witness-box. Did all this mean, he wondered, that it was the man standing there who had driven Julie to her death?

Ray Mercury took the oath quickly and began answering the Coroner's questions with what appeared to be complete sincerity. Phil, trying to look at the man dispassionately had to admit it, he certainly had good looks, plus his magnetic personality. Slumping dispiritedly in his seat, Phil could not help deciding that Mercury must have a certain attraction for women.

'She was employed by you at this club, the Black Moth. Would you say she was happy there?'

'She seemed to me to be happy.'

'You were friendly with her?'

'I am friendly with all my employees.'

'Evidence has been given to the effect that Miss Grayson died from poison, self-administered, which was probably contained in a capsule. Can you give the court any idea how such a thing could come into her possession?'

'Why, no.' Mercury flashed very white teeth. 'I'm a night-club owner, not a chemist.' He said it quietly and without any hint of sarcasm, yet there was a sudden steeliness in his tone which was unmistakable. He was making it quite clear, Phil decided, that no one was going to get away with the faintest imputation against him.

'You can throw no light on it?' the Coroner said. 'We have learned that Miss Grayson had not been happy lately.'

'I had understood that from her, and I can only imagine it was why she had left my employment.'

'She left your club at which she was working?'

'She left about a week ago.'

'Did she give any reason?'

There was a little silence. Still Mercury had appeared not to be aware of Thelma. Now he spoke slowly. 'I can only think,' he said, 'that she went because I told her that I didn't reciprocate the attachment she had lately formed for me.'

'She had formed an attachment for you?'

'Yes, I'm afraid she had. I couldn't help it, it was just one of those things.'

'Miss Grayson was infatuated with you, that is what you are saying?'

He nodded. 'I suppose you could call it that. I was willing to be on friendly terms with her. I liked her, she was a very sweet girl. But that was all there was to it, so far as I was concerned.'

'So after you told her this, she decided to leave?'

'That was the way of it.'

The Coroner turned to Thelma. 'Miss Grayson,' he said, 'no, you need not come to the witness-box. You knew of this infatuation your sister had for Mr. Mercury?'

'Yes,' she said. Almost a whisper it was.

'When she left the club she went to Little Tiplow?'

'Yes. I encouraged her to go to the cottage. I thought it would help her to think things over, to see it all in a different perspective. I hoped she would forget this . . . him.'

Phil saw her face was enigmatic, her tone expressionless as she glanced briefly at the man in the witness-box. And now he was regarding her, as if he was seeing her for the first time, one dark eyebrow raised in slight surprise.

'And you continued to remain in Mr. Mercury's employ?'

Thelma nodded.

'There was no reason why she shouldn't,' Mercury said. 'Miss Thelma Grayson is a sensible girl, she's in show-business and good at her job. And there was no need for her to be affected by her sister's decision.'

Thelma made no reply. She stood looking at the Coroner. She might not have heard what the man in the witness-box had said. Tension flickered round the Court like invisible lightning.

'Thank you, Miss Grayson, that is all.'

Thelma sat down, Phil looking at her curiously, a dozen questions spinning round in his mind.

The Coroner regarded Ray Mercury for a moment, then he thanked him for his evidence, and the man left the witness-box and took a seat at the back of the court.

The Coroner turned his gaze to the jury. 'You have heard all the evidence,' he told the eleven impassive faces, 'and I don't think I need go over it all again. You have listened carefully to the witnesses, I am sure, and it is quite plain how this unfortunate girl met her death. She was young, impressionable, and had formed an unfortunate attachment which was not reciprocated. An attachment which has been frankly explained to you, for which no blame can be attributed to anyone. How far this emotional situation contributed to the deceased's state of mind at the time of her death, is for you to say.' He touched briefly on the evidence of the two doctors, Dr. Walsh and Dr. Edwards. He referred to the evidence consistent with Julie Grayson having administered cyanide to herself by means of a capsule; he came to the end of his summing-up. 'Was she so worried and tormented, emotionally unstable at the time, that she decided to take her own life? That is what you have to decide. Will you please retire and consider your verdict?'

The jury rose and filed out of the room, their footsteps making a sharp clatter as they crossed the hall into a room opposite. It seemed only a short wait before the noise of their footsteps returned and they filed back into their places.

'Members of the jury, have you considered your verdict?'

The foreman rose, his red face grim. 'Yes, sir. We find that the deceased, Julie Grayson, killed herself while the balance of her mind was disturbed.'

Chapter Seven

The rakish-looking, low-built, yellow Duesenberg drew up outside the Weir Hotel, and Miss Frayle and Dr. Morelle got out of the car. The hotel was a modern building, low and somewhat Spanish in style with a wide veranda running round it. It was a warm afternoon, and the sun was shining on the white hotel walls.

Miss Frayle glanced at the lawn, its green faded to patching browns by the hot summer that was ending, which sloped down to the river. Beyond some trees she could see the water pouring over the weir in a cascade of froth. Her eyes travelled across the river to the old church, which stood almost opposite close to the water's edge, shaded from the sunlight by yew trees, dark and sombre.

'That looks like it, Dr. Morelle,' she said.

Dr. Morelle turned at the door of the hotel and looked in the direction Miss Frayle was pointing. His hooded gaze rested on the tiny church for a few moments. 'That we shall ascertain after we have had some tea,' he said.

He pushed open the glazed door and followed Miss Frayle into the hotel. Presently she and Dr. Morelle found themselves in a corner of the lounge, with tea being set before them.

Dr. Morelle's visit to Hatford was on account of several reports which had lately reached him, concerning the grave of a well-known author of criminological works, who had died some five years before. His name was Professor Kerr, and according to these reports his grave had fallen into disrepair, and had become very neglected.

Dr. Morelle had been aware that the professor had no family or relatives, although there had been one or two friends whom he had understood were supposed to have been responsible for the upkeep of the grave. He had made a number of inquiries among people who had known Kerr in London, but could obtain no satisfactory information. The result was that he had decided to investigate the matter for himself.

Dr. Morelle and Professor Kerr had been good friends, they had worked together on one or two scientific papers. Kerr had been a great admirer of

Dr. Morelle, and though their paths had separated towards the end of the former's life, and they had seen each other infrequently, Dr. Morelle had always held a warm place in his heart for his former colleague.

So on this bright late September afternoon, Dr. Morelle, accompanied by Miss Frayle, had turned the long bonnet of the Duesenberg out of Harley Street and westwards past Kew, through Staines and along the road towards Basingstoke, and into Hampshire beside a river, along which ran woods whose green was beginning to turn to bronze, and so to the little market town of Hatford.

The church where Professor Kerr was buried was, so Dr. Morelle had been informed, on the other side of the river across the old narrow suspension bridge; there the grave was, in the tiny churchyard. The Weir Hotel where Dr. Morelle had stopped for tea lay back from the road a few yards before reaching the bridge.

After their tea Dr. Morelle and Miss Frayle went out of the hotel and walked over a narrow footbridge which ran beside the suspension bridge. The sun was dipping behind the wooded hills as they came over the bridge, turned right and entered the churchyard.

It was an old Norman-towered church, overgrown with ivy and creeper; the churchyard itself was ragged with tall grass and seemed only adequately well-kept, almost every tombstone and gravestone was covered with moss, so that the names on them were almost always undecipherable.

Dr. Morelle and Miss Frayle walked round the churchyard trying to see a stone which by its comparatively new appearance might mark the spot where Professor Kerr lay buried. Although they searched carefully among the graves, there was no sign of the one which Dr. Morelle was seeking.

Presently he and Miss Frayle turned away from the graveyard, and went into the church itself. Outside a woman's bicycle leaned against the wall, but inside the church there was no one to be found whom they could ask for information concerning the whereabouts of the professor's last resting-place.

Dr. Morelle and Miss Frayle stood for some moments in the cool gloom of the church. The air was heavy with the scent of incense as they looked around, hoping to find some reference to the particular grave in the church records, but there was nothing to help them. Presently they went out into the early evening.

Dr. Morelle was recalling again that the information he had gone on in London had not been completely reliable, it was only surmise which had prompted him to seek out this church on the river-bank at Hatford. A frown darkened his gaunt face and his lips were tight with determination. He was making up his mind that he would not return to London until his quest was successfully concluded. What had started off as an errand of respect for a dead colleague had now become a challenge to his perseverance.

'Shouldn't we go back to the hotel,' Miss Frayle said. She could not refrain a faint sigh, this was hardly her idea of spending a nice late summer evening, mooching around old churchyards, looking for a lost grave. She had seen Dr. Morelle's face and read his expression correctly. 'I believe,' she went on, 'that there is a place near called Little Tiplow, and it was suggested by someone in London, I can't remember who it was, that Professor Kerr might be buried there.'

Dr. Morelle recollected that his old friend had, in fact, lived in the village of Little Tiplow at the time of his death.

'That notion had already occurred to me,' he said. 'We might find someone at the hotel who could put us on the right track.'

They went back the way they had come, over the narrow footbridge across the river. They stood for a minute watching the boats passing underneath, a slim, fragile-looking racing skiff flashed by, a motor-boat chugged slowly below in the opposite direction. Further down the stream Miss Frayle watched a white swan move lazily over the green waters. Dusk was beginning to fall and Miss Frayle drew her light coat about her against the chill in the air, now that the sun had gone.

Back in the hotel, Dr. Morelle found the cashier behind the inquiries desk, she was a middle-aged woman, and he asked her if she knew anything about the grave concerned. She was unable to help him, but as Dr. Morelle turned away he came face-to-face with an old waiter, at the same moment that the woman behind the desk, seeing him, asked him if he had any information which could help Dr. Morelle.

'Yes,' the old chap said. 'I remember him being buried down here, he used to live nearby. But it wasn't at that church,' he waved the tray he was carrying in the direction of the river, 'it was the church over at Little Tiplow where he was buried.'

Little Tiplow was a tiny village about two miles distant, and Dr. Morelle and Miss Frayle got into the Duesenberg and drove over the bridge and through the town. Dr. Morelle had switched on the car's side lights, street-lamps came alight and lights were popping in the shops and windows of the houses as dusk fell over Hatford.

Some minutes later the Duesenberg swung past Hatford Station and went on through the station yard, and continued along another road which wound uphill a short distance. Dr. Morelle turned into a rough-surfaced lane, and after about a hundred yards the lane turned left into a wider road and the car sped on past an old inn, where a light was swinging from underneath its sign.

Miss Frayle couldn't catch the name of the inn, though she screwed up her eyes behind her horn-rimmed glasses. She remembered the old waiter when he was directing Dr. Morelle to the churchyard, mentioning that the road went past an inn on the right. So Dr. Morelle was on the right road, not that she expected him to have mistaken his way, she reflected. It was not like Dr. Morelle to get lost.

The Duesenberg swung onto the road for Little Tiplow. Fields stretched away into the distance, the evening mist was beginning to come up from the river, and drift across like a company of wraiths and into the woods over on the right. Now the Duesenberg's great headlamps were switched on and their twin powerful beams sliced the night.

Presently to their left rose up a dark cluster of trees. 'That is Witches' Wood,' Dr. Morelle told Miss Frayle, and chuckled a little to himself as he felt her shudder.

They turned into a long, gloomy tunnel which ran under a railway, and which seemed to continue through the hillside for about half-a-mile. The car's headlamps bored through the darkness and the echo of its engines came back eerily to Miss Frayle's ears. She murmured a prayer of thanks when they were out of it, and driving up the road ahead, which was now pale in the gloom.

They turned again, until they were running along another road which lay parallel with the river. It gleamed darkly and they passed a cottage on the bank, with a large flat-bottomed boat moored alongside. This was Mill Ferry, Miss Frayle presumed, and once again recalling that the waiter at the hotel had mentioned it. Once again she marvelled to herself at the manner in which Dr. Morelle had kept on the route he'd been given.

Further on she could see the mill itself, rising tall and gaunt. They left it on their right, and now they were heading for Little Tiplow itself.

Little Tiplow turned out to be composed of only a mere handful of houses and a church. Lights were gleaming behind the curtains of the cottage-windows as the Duesenberg's headlights swept through the village and pulled up outside the lych-gate of the church, low-built and greyish against the night sky.

Dr. Morelle took a large torch from underneath the dashboard and they made their way to the gate in the shadow of its porch. At first it appeared to be locked, and then Dr. Morelle gave one end a push and it swung open on its axis in the centre, the other end nearly knocking Miss Frayle off her feet. Slowly, in the increasing darkness, Miss Frayle followed Dr. Morelle into the churchyard. Some gravestones shimmered palely; somewhere an owl was hooting. There was no moon, only the light of the torch to guide them, as they made their way around the churchyard. Miss Frayle stumbled over old gravestones, and found herself a trifle hysterically apologizing, as if those who lay beneath might be disturbed by her jumping on them. Here again the graves were very old and covered with moss, and the names mostly indecipherable.

Then Miss Frayle gave a cry and pointed to what appeared to be a comparatively new gravestone caught in the circle of light from the torch.

'Dr. Morelle,' she said, 'perhaps that's it.'

Dr. Morelle went forward and now they saw that it was a large stone tilted towards their gaze. Unfortunately, however, the inscription on it read: Colonel Somebody-or-Other of the Scots Guards, and a very martial-looking sword could be seen above the inscription.

Miss Frayle uttered a groan of disappointment which turned to a gasp of terror. In the darkness she suddenly felt something pushing against her ankle. She recoiled, but managed to force her glance downwards. It was a tubby grey cat brushing against her, purring loudly, its eyes gleaming yellow up at her. Miss Frayle smiled to herself at her timid fears, and bent and stroked the cat.

She followed Dr. Morelle along the path back to the Duesenberg, and then Dr. Morelle saw a shadowy figure coming out from behind the vicarage which stood next to the church. It was a man who came into view and Dr. Morelle paused to ask the newcomer if he knew if the man they sought was buried in the churchyard.

In the light from Dr. Morelle's torch Miss Frayle saw that the man's hair was well slicked down, and he was wearing a collar and tie, obviously, she decided, on his way to a local dance, or to the village inn for an evening's amusement. At once he answered Dr. Morelle's query.

'Yes, I do remember the name; but he's not buried here. I think you'll find his grave in the cemetery. That's new, leastways only ten years old or so, it's on the other side of the village.'

He spoke with a pleasant burr, and as he finished there was a movement behind him, and another figure approached. He was a farm-labourer, and he confirmed what Dr. Morelle had just been told. The two men directed Dr. Morelle, the cemetery was about only a mile away it seemed, and he got into the car, Miss Frayle beside him.

He reversed the Duesenberg, the two men watching him with interest, then he set off back through the village. Miss Frayle was beginning to feel she'd had enough of graveyards for one evening, a cloud of increasingly dark depression was descending upon her, but she knew that any protest on her part would go unheeded by the saturnine figure beside her at the steering-wheel.

They came to the beginning of what was no more than a cart-track, with wire-fencing either side.

The moon had appeared low on the horizon, stars were beginning to twinkle in the sky. Dr. Morelle decided to stop the car, he was not quite sure of the condition of the way ahead, and so he switched off the engine and the headlights, and with Miss Frayle hanging onto his arm, he set off.

There were two or three houses on either side of the cart-track, but still no sign of any cemetery. They came to a fork in the path, and with the idea that it looked the least rough of the two, Dr. Morelle took the right-hand fork. He and Miss Frayle went on for about fifty yards, and then a door of a cottage opened, and a man's shadow appeared in the lighted doorway.

'Are we right for the cemetery?' Dr. Morelle asked.

Dr. Morelle and Miss Frayle could feel the man's eyes on them, and there was a moment's hesitation before he answered.

'No, you're coming the wrong way,' the man said. 'You should have taken the other fork.'

They returned the way they had come, and then took the left-hand fork, Dr. Morelle leading the way with the torch he had brought from the car, Miss Frayle close behind him, fearful she would lose him in the darkness. It was a rough track, riddled with cart-tracks, until suddenly it opened out into a small space, beyond which was a low gate. They went through the gate, and there they could dimly see the white shapes of recent gravestones.

How were they to find which was the grave they wanted? Miss Frayle wondered. Everywhere the gravestones seemed to look alike. Then Miss Frayle heard a voice saying something about someone having left some flowers. It was a woman's voice, Dr. Morelle had heard it too, and he called out: 'Could you tell me which is Professor Kerr's grave? I believe he is buried here.'

There was a pause and then a squat, dumpy shape waddled out of the shadows. In the darkness they could make out the pale blob of a face with a wide smile, and a head covered in some sort of a black shawl. It was the same woman's voice they had just heard that came to them now out of the gloom. Beyond her, Miss Frayle could make out another figure, no doubt that was who they had heard the woman talking to.

'Yes,' the dumpy woman said. 'He's here; if you like to follow me, I'll show you where it is.'

Dr. Morelle thanked her for her trouble, the woman said it was no trouble at all, she was only too glad to show him where the grave was. As Dr. Morelle followed Miss Frayle and the square woman down the path there was a sudden movement, and a figure rose up from the side of a grave.

Instinctively Dr. Morelle turned the beam of his torch on the figure and in its light saw it was a dark-eyed, pale beautiful girl. She had obviously been kneeling at a grave. Dr. Morelle paused, as if he had the impression that she was about to speak to him, Miss Frayle thought. She too was impressed by the girl's face. But the girl said nothing, and Dr. Morelle went on, Miss Frayle behind him.

'Here it is,' the woman said, a few moments later. She pointed to a white cross that stood behind a neat rectangle of gravel. On the cross was the professor's name, suitably inscribed, and the date of his birth and death.

Dr. Morelle questioned the woman and ascertained from her that the grave was, in fact, kept in good order, occasionally someone from Little Tiplow who had known Professor Kerr there, came over from time to time and put flowers on the grave. Dr. Morelle was completely reassured that there was no basis for the reports that Professor Kerr's last resting-place was a patch of overgrown weeds, neglected and forgotten.

Miss Frayle had by now lost interest in the grave, though she was glad that Dr. Morelle had finally found it, and that all was well with it; she was, in fact, much more intrigued by the young woman they had seen rising up from beside the grave at which she had been kneeling. Miss Frayle longed to ask the squat, dumpy woman with the odd shawl hood over her round face, about the girl. Who was she? Why was she there so late, in the darkness? Was it because she had become recently bereaved that she was there, praying at the grave of someone dear to her?

But Miss Frayle asked the woman none of these things. Instead, she remained silent and after they had said good night to the woman she and Dr. Morelle returned to the car. Dr. Morelle expressed his satisfaction with the outcome of their journey as the Duesenberg bumped along the rough cart-track to the road. Miss Frayle murmured appropriately in reply.

But as the Duesenberg headed through the village, on through Hatford and across the suspension-bridge, past the strings of gaily-coloured lights which now ornamented the Weir Hotel and were reflected in the river, Miss Frayle could still see on the screen of her mind the face of the girl in the graveyard.

The car sped on to London, but Miss Frayle found she could not dismiss the girl's haunting face from her thoughts.

Chapter Eight

Thelma Grayson stirred at the window. Down in the street the fat, bald proprietor of the little restaurant opposite was bowing a party of late patrons to the door, now the lights began to dim behind the net curtains as the shadows of the waiters moved around, clearing up. Presently, the glaring neon sign over the door went out.

The sitting-room of the Charlotte Street flat was almost in darkness now, without the red and blue flashes from the neon that had shone on Thelma's white face, set in taut, tragic lines, her long eyes grey haunted pools.

She had been there in the darkness, without realizing the passing hours, now she switched on a standard-lamp and drew the curtains. The evening was beginning to end in Charlotte Street. Further down, across Oxford Street where the environs of Soho sprawled untidily, the night was young.

She moved to a little writing-desk in the corner, and as she bent to the drawer her eyes met those of Julie staring at her, luminous and smiling, from the leather-framed photograph. Thelma hesitated momentarily, then her gaze went down to the drawer she had opened. She took out the revolver.

It was cold to the touch of her pale slender fingers. It glinted up at her evilly, silky smooth and bluish-black. It was a Smith and Wesson Centennial, hammerless and pumping a .38 calibre cartridge. It wasn't the newest pattern, made of all-aluminium alloy. It was quite heavy in her hand.

She put on a short cashmere coat which had been lying over the back of a chair, and she slipped the gun into the right hand pocket and she switched out the light and quietly left the flat.

She walked purposefully along Charlotte Street, the way she had taken many times before to the Black Moth, she and Julie. Until lately, when she had made her own way while Julie had been down at Lilac Cottage. Now Julie would not accompany her ever again.

Julie with her amused laugh and inconsequential gossip, who would always pause to talk to any stray cat appearing out of the shadows, as one had appeared now, a thin-looking creature which shot across her path and into the road, escaping destruction by a swiftly-moving taxi by the merest tip of its crooked tail.

She could feel the hard pressure of the revolver in her pocket as she walked on past the café on the corner where olive-skinned men lounged in the garish electric light over their cups of coffee. She passed a brilliantly-lit shop where a fat woman was sweeping up, a cigarette drooping from the corner of her mouth.

Only subconsciously was she aware of what was happening about her. From the corner of her eye she glimpsed the Scala Theatre, its foyer darkened, the bills outside announcing some musical play being performed there. Further on across the road a group of men rocked on their heels on the kerb outside a public house, deep in animated conversation. The lights of a restaurant flickered in red and blue above half a dozen cars, one of which drew off, its occupants in evening clothes.

She passed the familiar scenes of broken buildings and empty spaces and masses of scaffolding reaching up to the night sky, rebuilding that was going on interminably. On either side as she passed ran the colourful miscellany of shops and offices, restaurants and cafés. Tailors and dry-cleaners, delicatessen-shops, jewellers and pawnbrokers. Now she was passing a German café, its windows packed with liver sausages and *sauerkraut*.

On the other side of the road a taxi was pulling up before a Greek restaurant, and two men and two women hurried in to supper behind the pink-lighted windows. Names of half a dozen different nationalities adorned the shop fronts and café signs on either side of her. In an Italian coffee-bar the white blobs of faces in a golden haze beyond the windows bent over cups, or were illuminated for a moment in the flame of a cigarette-lighter. A car purred silently past, with a peaked-cap chauffeur at the wheel, its passenger a solitary figure deep in the cushions of one corner.

Taxis hurried along picking up fares, or dropping them, at their different rendezvous. Dark-skinned men padded past her, sometimes alone, sometimes in pairs, and she could sense their black, bold eyes on her face, the aroma of their cigarettes hung on the air after them. She passed alleys and culs-de-sac where figures moved in the shadows, and where a stray cat or dog sneaked silently among the garbage.

Overhead the night sky glowed with the reflection of the lights of Oxford Street and Piccadilly. Bits of newspaper and refuse littered the gutter and was strewn about the pavement, the variegated smells of cooking and rich spices came to her nostrils, but Thelma Grayson's senses, while they registered all these sights and sounds and odours about her, retained them only briefly, her every thought was fixed upon the recent past. The Coroner's pince-nez glinting in the morning sunlight. The faces of the jury as they sat listening to the witnesses following one another into the witness-box in that drab, bare room; Phil Stone's troubled brow as he sat next to her.

Phil had accompanied her to the cemetery at Little Tiplow, they had been the only mourners, though a few villagers had put in an appearance out of ghoulish interest. The funeral had taken place the next day following the inquest, a grey morning until the moment when the coffin was being lowered into the grave, when sunshine had suddenly broken through, bringing to life the flowers at the graveside, in all their colour and beauty. Flowers from Thelma and Phil, and from the girls with whom Julie had worked at the Black Moth.

There had been a huge wreath of roses from Ray Mercury, which Phil had scowled at. Reading his unspoken thoughts Thelma had said to him: 'Julie would have liked them in spite of everything, in spite of who sent them.'

She recalled the savage intensity of his tone as he said to her later: 'Why didn't you tell me?'

'Was it for me to tell you about him? I wanted Julie to do that.'

'That was why you wanted me to hurry down to the cottage?'

'I felt that after she had seen you again it would work out all right for you both. I thought she had got over him, I never dreamed she would do what she did.'

'He killed her,' Phil had said, 'he drove her to do what she did.'

She had seen the expression in his face, an expression which had chilled her, and she had forced a note of calm and common-sense into her voice. It was when they were returning to London in the train three days after the funeral, the sunlight which had broken through in the morning had stayed to fill the sky, and the brightness of the fields and gardens racing past mocked their sadness. Phil was remembering the train journey he had made on that evening from London to Hatford, the excitement with which the prospect of seeing Julie again had filled him. He was remembering the vision of her face which had filled his mind. Now that picture was obliterated by that other face which try as he would he could not prevent returning to his mind, Julie's face as he had last seen her.

Hers and another face, Ray Mercury's, soft and withdrawn and secret, as he had stood in the witness-box answering the questions put to him by the Coroner with an air of deepest sincerity.

'You mustn't feel that way about him,' Thelma had said to him. They were alone in the compartment, sitting in opposite corner seats. She could see the whiteness of his knuckles as his fingers entwined in a tense grip. 'He had nothing to do with it.'

'How can you defend him?' he had said, his voice rasping. 'I know I sound jealous of him. I admit it, I am. But it isn't confusing me so that I don't know she killed herself because he had let her down. It's as obvious as hell.'

'That isn't true,' she had tried her utmost to sound convincing. 'She was infatuated with him, of course.' She had broken off as she saw the spasm of anguish that twisted his face. 'Oh, Phil, it was an infatuation, she didn't love him, and if only you had been around it would never have happened.'

'Why did she have to kill herself?'

'That's something we shall never know.'

Phil had looked at her, but could read nothing that told him anything in the expression at the back of her eyes.

A long silence had fallen between them as the train rushed on towards London, and they were left each possessed by their own thoughts, their faces turned unseeingly to the windows.

Thelma had found herself recalling the incident last night, when she was at the cemetery putting fresh flowers on the grave, and she had been disturbed by the arrival of two visitors, a tall man and a woman, she had received the impression that the woman was small and the fluffy type. She had caught the glint of her horn-rimmed glasses in the reflection from the torch-beam which the man had shone on her. She recalled the man's voice, quiet and incisive and the woman's light and sounding a little timorous, as they had moved on. She was idly wondering who they were, and what they had been doing there at the cemetery at that late hour. Then her thoughts trailed off, to fasten to another picture, that of the smooth-faced man in the witness-box, and her grey eyes became veiled.

Phil had shared her taxi, which had dropped him at his rooms near Baker Street, while she had gone on to Charlotte Street, Phil arranging to telephone her the following day, and arrange for them to meet. She had realized how lonely he was, and how he was numbed by the shock of Julie's death.

This was yesterday afternoon when they had come back to London. Following the funeral, Thelma had returned to Lilac Cottage where she had remained, tidying up, while Phil had stayed on at the Half Moon in the village, though he had called on Thelma for an hour or two each day at the cottage.

Thelma had shut up the cottage with all its memories locked in it, not knowing when, she felt, she would ever be able to return to it. She had decided, she told Phil, that she did not expect to come back to Lilac Cottage for several months. They had driven over in a hired car to Hatford Station, where they had caught the train to Waterloo.

Now Thelma found herself out of Charlotte Street, and crossing over to Bateman Street. She passed a bookshop, its windows packed with paper-backed novels in several languages. Romances in French, thrillers in German, and American-style dramas.

Across the other side of the darkened street ran a length of corrugated iron fencing, behind which lay another gap which had been torn out of London by war-time bombs.

She could feel again the hard pressure of the revolver in her coat pocket, and she directed her thoughts towards what lay ahead of her. A few yards away was the glitter and garish colours of night-time Oxford Street.

So intent was she on the purpose for which she had set out, that she stepped into the gutter in Oxford Street, and only the loud hooting from a taxi caused her to draw back in time to avert an accident.

Thelma Grayson paused and collected her thoughts focusing them on the present, and here and now, and she crossed Oxford Street and turned into Soho Street. The clamour and colour and movement of Oxford Street formed a brief distraction, but she was in a shadowed street again, and her thoughts turned inwards as before.

She turned right into Soho Square, great trees overhanging the square through which glittered the lights of Hollywood film companies. She skirted the square and went down into Frith Street. Now the atmosphere was similar to that of Charlotte Street, except that there seemed to be a brightly-lit café or restaurant every step of the way. Here again olive-skinned faces peered at her, one man paused as he was smoking a long cigarette, made as if to move after her, but then he caught her expression and remained where he was.

Women, heavily made-up and teetering on high heels, flitted in the shadows like vultures, groups of men hung about in the doorways of shops and office entrances.

Now she was approaching the end of her journey and her pace slackened, the feverish suspense which had racked her began to fall away, now she knew she would have to whip her flagging spirits if she was to force herself to do that which she had set out that night to do.

She crossed over and paused on the corner of Meard Street, and went a few yards along before she turned into another street, narrow and dark, where she saw ahead of her the familiar neon sign jutting out above the pavement. The shape of a black moth picked out in crimson neon, its eyes flashing on and off, and over it the name: The Black Moth in green and yellow.

Cars and taxis were drawing up to set down visitors to the club, and behind the vehicles she could see the stalwart, saluting figure of the commissionaire in his opulent-looking uniform. Quickly she crossed over to the other side of the street, and made her way along, turning her face away from the club so that she might not be observed. She passed the club with its bustle of arrivals, then crossed back again to the same side. Facing her was an alley, black and cavernous, beyond it she knew was a yard, upon which opened an entrance to the Black Moth.

She went quickly down the alley and into the darkness of the yard. Something slithered past her in the blackness, so that she halted, a gasp starting at the back of her throat and bitten off before she could utter it aloud. It might have been a rat or a cat; more likely a rat, she thought. She went on.

There were no lights in the yard, only a glow from a window above her to the left, and for a moment she halted to get her bearings. She made out the iron staircase that led to the door to a passage, which in turn led to Ray Mercury's private office, at the back of the club. She had the key to the door in the pocket of the blouse she wore. The revolver banged against her thigh, hard and sinister as she went up the iron stairs, the soft scuffing noise of her shoes was the only sound as she reached the door.

Chapter Nine

Next thing he had to do, Ray Mercury was thinking, was to get rid of him. He was smiling gently, while he was thinking, at the man who was opposite him. His eyes were smiling too at Luke's little joke. So that Luke let the thin strip of moustache above his mouth curl back in a laugh. He was getting fonder of telling his jokes, and laughing more loudly at them, than anyone else.

Yes, Ray Mercury was thinking, that was the next thing he had to do, get rid of Luke.

He began to turn over in his mind what would be the best way, leaning back in the large padded chair behind his ornately carved writing-desk. Luke was pacing slowly up and down, casting an appraising eye at the richly furnished room that was the boss's office at the back of the Black Moth Club; that was in between his jokes.

Ray Mercury's double-breasted dinner-jacket of midnight blue fitted perfectly, and his silk shirt with its turned-down collar was immaculately white. It was tough on him, he was thinking, eyeing Luke speculatively, that he'd been forced to use him this way with the Grayson girl; but he'd had to work quickly before she had time to open that pretty mouth of hers. Yes, it had been tough on him to have to do that, to make Luke a partner in a murder, and it would now be tough on Luke. Already he'd sensed the change in the other's attitude, he seemed to have put himself on a basis of equality, instead of that of a well-paid henchman. Ray Mercury's experience of men of Luke's type warned him that if ever the time came he would try to do one of two things, either squeak to the police, or fix him, in a way that it would look accidental. Or that he had committed suicide, the way Julie Grayson had been fixed. He laughed mirthlessly to himself.

Although his office was only a short distance from the head of the stairs leading to the club itself, no sound reached them, no sound of dance-music or anything. The door and walls were sound-proofed. Ray Mercury liked to have complete silence to think in, to plan and scheme.

Now he watched Luke's eyes as they took in the thick, deep crimson carpet, the sumptuous cocktail-cabinet, the television-set in the corner, the book-lined shelves, the gleam of highly-polished furniture, the aroma of his expensive cigar, all the trappings which went with the owner of one of London's smartest and most luxurious nightclubs. Ray Mercury could see not only appreciation in the other's eyes, those eyes that were like two bits of grey slate, but something else lurked there, envy and greed. And he knew that Luke was already fancying himself as the boss.

As he sighed to himself, the crystal door-handle turned, and the door opened, and a woman came in.

'Hello, Greta,' Ray Mercury said.

He did not often see his wife these days. She did not smile at him or answer him. She just stood there by the door glancing at Luke.

'All right, Luke,' Ray Mercury said.

After a moment's hesitation the other took the hint and with a smirk at the woman in the doorway, he went past her and closed the door behind him.

Greta Mercury came into the room and he idly admired her graceful figure in the tightly-fitting dress she was wearing. Still a good-looker, he thought. Her hair, silvery blonde, still rippled down to her shoulders and was as lovely as it had been when she had first attracted him in Hamburg. That was where he had met her, just after the war had ended and he had been engaged in highly lucrative, if dubious and dangerous operations in that part of the world, her smooth shoulders rose white and rounded from the revealing dress.

Maybe, he thought, her eyes, those strangely green slanting eyes were a little harder now. Maybe that the line about her mouth was a little tauter. But what had she to complain of? She had nothing to worry her now, she had done all right for herself, since he had picked her up in that Hamburg night-club, she ought to know that.

'Hello, Ray,' she said, speaking for the first time, in her hoarse voice, which had once excited him with its slow, controlled tone. Even when he had seen her quivering with fury and passion he had never heard her speak without the icy composure with which she spoke now. Only the green fires in her eyes and the whitening at the corners of her mouth betrayed her emotions.

He didn't say anything. There wasn't much to find to say to her these days. He tapped the ash of the long cigar into the big, gleaming ash-tray on his desk.

'I've been thinking you don't see me around so much,' she said.

'Come and have a drink now you're here,' he said.

She shook her head. She moved forward towards the desk and he saw the glitter in her green eyes, like sunlight in an icy cavern.

'I've been thinking lately,' she said.

'So that's what's been the matter,' he said. He tried to make it light, but seeing the expression on her face he did not altogether succeed.

'If you want to know something, you're just a great big kid, who can't help falling for the newest pretty shape and face.'

So this was it, the familiar stuff. He shrugged his beautifully-tailored broad shoulders. 'It's the way I'm made,' he said. 'Anyway, is that all the conversation you have to offer? What are you worrying about? You have money, clothes, a lovely flat, you can go wherever you want to go, Paris, Cannes, Nice, you have the world at your feet; and yet you worry because now and again I like to play around with a new toy.'

'That sounds all right to you from where you're standing,' she said. 'But it doesn't make me feel so good. Because one of these days you'll find a toy that you'll want to keep for keeps. You won't want it just for play-time only.'

'I'll never finish with you, darling,' he said, and he moved round the desk towards her. He moved lightly, quietly, and his voice was soft as he stepped forward to her and his carefully manicured hands held her shoulders.

It was strange, he was thinking, that she did not stir him any more; and he was thinking of those old days not so many years ago, he was recalling the fire that had been in her embrace. That strange icy beauty of hers was a façade behind which he had soon discovered lay smouldering volcanic flames. That was what had been the trouble, he supposed, the fire had burnt itself out too soon. Or maybe it was just that what had appealed to him then, now had no impact at all.

'You're my wife, and you're going to stay my wife,' he said smoothly. 'We've had good times together, Greta, and don't forget that. What else, as I've said to you before, what else do you want from me?'

'Maybe happiness,' she said.

His eyes were narrowing. 'What's got into you? What's started you taking this slant on me? Why suddenly, you haven't worried about it before? Why this aggrieved act lately?'

'Maybe something to do with that Grayson girl,' she said.

'That poor kid,' he said.

'Yes,' she said. 'That poor kid.'

He exhaled a cloud of cigar-smoke slowly, watched it curl above her pale hair.

'She got so infatuated with you she had to go and kill herself, very flattering for you. But what do you think I felt when I read all that stuff in the newspapers? That stuff you said at the inquest, you being so modest and so attractive, but forcing yourself to admit it, that some damned girl fell for you, and because you don't bother to look at her, she goes and takes poison. What do you think I feel about that? I'm telling you, Ray, one of these days you won't be quite so eager to drop one of these girls. And I won't ever see you again.'

'You're out of your mind,' he said. 'I tell you I couldn't help it; it wasn't because she was infatuated with me, but because she was that sort of girl. I tell you, I couldn't help it at all.'

'You're lying, Ray, you rat,' she said.

She was smiling softly as she said it, but he stepped back as if she had struck him a physical blow. She waited, seeing the malicious glitter in his eyes, and the colour rise to his soft, pale face.

'I don't like anyone to call me that,' he said, his voice was thick. 'I don't like it from anybody, not even you, Greta.'

He moved away slowly back to his desk, drawing deeply on his cigar. She saw his eyes looking at her speculatively through the cigar-smoke. She stood quite still. She didn't move after him.

'Maybe it'll be a bit of a warning to you, Ray,' she said. 'The Grayson girl was the last straw. I'm warning you, keep your private life private, don't let it get public so that I can feel the few friends I have laughing at me behind my back.'

He smiled at her, as the cloud of cigar-smoke cleared, and she could see his face. 'Thank you for the tip-off, Greta,' he said. 'If that's all you've got to say you can get along back home. I must go and talk to my customers, and keep them amused. After all,' he could not resist saying, 'it's through them you can have those trips to Paris, the clothes you are wearing and the perfume you are using. And don't worry, Greta, I'm not going to let anyone else get me. You are so nice, Greta,' he said, 'to come home to.'

She stood at the door for a moment staring at him with those green eyes, no longer aflame now, but steady and cold. Then without a word she opened the door and went out.

As she closed the door Ray Mercury thought he caught a glimpse of Luke further along the passage, in an attitude as if he had been waiting for her.

Ray Mercury sat down at his desk, dragging thoughtfully at his cigar. The way she had acted to-night, that had come as a considerable shock to him. He hadn't realized that she was taking it so badly about his affairs with the girls at his club. He hadn't realized that she felt as she did about Julie Grayson. He wondered what she would do if she knew it wasn't suicide, that Julie hadn't been so infatuated with him that she wasn't ready to go and yap to the police about what she had discovered about him.

He sat there wrapped in his thoughts. He didn't look up when the door opened and he caught the sound of dance-music for a brief moment. He thought it was either Greta who had come back, or Luke. Not even when the door closed, shutting out the dance-music and the office was quiet again, cut off from the world the way he liked it, did he look up.

'Hello, Ray.'

It was only then that his head jerked up and he saw who it was standing there. He didn't get up, but sat staring at Thelma Grayson.

'This is an unexpected pleasure,' he said, one eyebrow raised.

'For you it may be.'

She came towards him, and he said: 'I didn't expect to see you back at the club yet. I imagined you would want to stay away for a few more days, after what happened.'

'Always so very considerate, aren't you?' she said. 'Julie was always telling me how considerate and thoughtful you were.'

He eyed her steadily. 'You know as well as I do that there was nothing I could have done about it,' he said. 'I didn't encourage her, it was just the way she felt for me.'

'You're a liar as well as a murderer,' she said.

He started and then realizing she could not know anything, that she was only talking dramatically, he regained his poise quickly. The hand that raised his cigar to his mouth did not tremble.

'You murdered her,' he heard her voice going on, 'Just as if you had strangled her with your own hands.'

She didn't know anything. She still thought that her sister had committed suicide, and a sense of lightness filled him. He started to get up from the desk, but she stopped him.

'Stay where you are,' she said. 'You don't have to stand up just because I come into the room. You can save your little gentleman's tricks.'

He sat still at his desk. 'Now listen, Thelma,' he said. 'You should get a grip on yourself. Julie's dead and I'm sorry about it.'

'I've been thinking about you,' she said, 'ever since I saw her in the mortuary. And I've been looking forward to this moment.'

'Incidentally, how the hell did you get in here?' he said. 'Who let you up?'

'Nobody,' she said. 'There's a key to that door to the yard at the back. I happened to get hold of it. Never mind how, I did. So nobody knows I'm here. Nobody saw me come in, nobody knows, Ray, except you and me. And only I will know when I go out.'

The tone in her voice suddenly sent a chill crawling under his scalp and down the back of his neck and down his spine. He rested his cigar on the edge of the ash-tray and he stood up from his chair.

'What is this? Tell me what you want and then get out.'

'It's not so much what I want,' she said. 'But what you are going to get.'

His mouth opened in disbelief as he saw the bluish-black glint of the revolver that had appeared in her hand. His voice was thick with the beginnings of fear now. 'Where did you get that damned gun?'

'All you have to worry about is how I'm going to use it,' she said. She moved forward a pace or two, the gun pointed at him, menacingly. 'Stay where you are. Right behind that nice big desk of yours.'

His face had turned a sickly grey, he could feel his legs trembling. He formed words in his throat, but could not force them to his stiff lips.

'Do you think you're going to scare me?' he heard himself say at last. 'You're not, Thelma. Don't be a damn fool, put that gun away.'

She did not say anything. He saw no change in her expression, and his voice faltered as he sought wildly for something else to say.

'Listen, I'm sorry about Julie. You know that. I didn't kill her, it was terrible for her, I know, it was terrible for you too, but —'

'And it's going to be terrible for you,' she said to him, between her teeth. 'I can see her face now, as it was in the mortuary. You should have seen it, Ray,' her voice rose with cold fury. 'You should have seen your handiwork, all contorted and twisted with agony, her face was.'

'Don't, Thelma,' he muttered hoarsely. 'Put that gun away and we'll talk —'

Again she interrupted him, but this time it was the gun that spoke. There was an explosion like a door slamming, only twenty times as loud it seemed, and Ray Mercury's eyes rolled upwards, and he stood there for a moment an expression of disbelief on his soft, white face, his mouth fell wide open. Then slowly he toppled forward and sprawled face downwards across the wide desk.

She stood staring at him, she put the Smith and Wesson slowly in her pocket and backed to the door. The gun going off must have sounded tremendously loud in the confined space of the room with its heavy, cigar-laden atmosphere, she thought.

She steeled herself for the noise of running feet, the shouts of alarm and the flinging open of the door. But there was no sound.

Stiffly and jerkily she turned to the door and opened it, there came the blare of dance-music, and she realized that only somebody standing right outside the door could have heard the shot in the sound-proof room. Without a glance behind her she went out of the office shutting the door. She walked along the passage to the iron staircase by which she had come. Nobody saw her, she closed the back door after her and she went down the steps quickly and silently into the darkness of the yard below.

Chapter Ten

For the rest of that day after he had returned to London, Phil Stone had drifted aimlessly around the town restless and dispirited, wondering what the future held for him, a future which seemed bleak and empty. He had gone as far as London Bridge, idly watching the shipping, the busy tugs and the swinging cranes. These were familiar sights to him and he found some comfort in the familiarity of the scene, it brought to him the breath of the sea, and gave him something solid and tangible for his thoughts to hang on to.

He went out to Deptford, past the docks and over Deptford Creek, and through Greenwich Foot Tunnel under the river to Cubitt Town and then back through a maze of streets to the ferry and over to Deptford again. Then on to Greenwich and the water front by the Royal Naval College, then to drift round the park, over to Blackheath, before heading back to the heart of London.

He had spent some time in his room in Baker Street, trying to read, to pass the hours with the newspapers, magazines and books, but he found it impossible to concentrate. All the time the words were jumbled before his eyes, as his thoughts continued to revolve round Julie and her death, and his mind dwelt on the life that might have been which he could have shared with her.

That evening of his return to London with Thelma Grayson, he went out to a nearby restaurant and ate a hurried meal, and then tried to lose himself in a cinema, but the figures on the screen and the voices that came to him meant nothing as he sat there in the darkness. It was only Julie's face he saw, it was only Julie's voice that he was remembering.

He found it unbearable, the stuffy, crowded darkness, and he hurried out to gulp the fresher air of the street. He roamed round the streets, went into one or two pubs. He avoided talking to anyone: he only wanted to be left alone with his deep grief.

Now he found himself in a little café in Greek Street, in the heart of Soho. He had just finished a meal of ravioli, and sat smoking a cigarette over a half-filled cup of coffee, he had been sitting there for a couple of hours. No one spoke to him here, no one tried to chat to him about the weather or anything else.

Now he knew all the time this was where his footsteps had been leading him. It was as if his wanderings had been nothing else but some subconscious effort to lead him to that very part of London which had kept drawing him like a compelling magnet. Drawing him closer, relentlessly drawing him to Soho. While all the time the conscious part of his brain had been urging him to keep away at all costs from that part of London where Ray Mercury and the Black Moth was.

On the bus, in the tube, while he had been in the cinema, or in his room trying to concentrate on a book or magazine, there had been at the back of his mind the memory of his conversation with Thelma Grayson in the train. He remembered the tone of her voice when she had tried to tell him that Ray Mercury had not been responsible for Julie's death, that he had not driven her to death as surely as if he had murdered her with his own hands.

He was remembering the huge wreath of roses which had arrived for Julie's coffin, and how he had hated the sight of the gorgeous flowers, he had struggled to prevent himself from tearing them to pieces; and how it was only Thelma telling him that Julie would have liked them that had prevented him from destroying them there and then.

'It was an infatuation,' he heard Thelma's voice telling him once more. 'She didn't love him, if only you had been around it would never have happened.' And then he remembered asking her why did she have to kill herself, and again her reply: 'That we shall never know.'

What had lain behind that hint of evasiveness in her tone? It reminded him of the way she had greeted him when he had first arrived at the Charlotte Street flat. Then she had tried to conceal from him her anxiety for Julie. She had not wanted him to know about Julie and Ray Mercury. But in the train it had seemed that she was not entirely convinced of what she had told him, it was as if she was trying to save him from bringing trouble upon himself. It was as if she was trying to keep him away from Ray Mercury the man who had destroyed the girl he loved.

He glanced at his wrist-watch, it was nearly eleven o'clock, he threw a look round the little café with the chatter of foreign voices all around him, and then he pushed back his half-empty cup of coffee, got up and paid his bill at the door and went out into Greek Street.

With a vague idea that the Black Moth was further down the street he went on purposefully. From the shadows a tight-skirted figure with swaying hips approached with her softly-spoken invitation, and he brushed past her.

He paused on a corner to speak to an olive-skinned man and ask him to direct him to the Black Moth Club. The man told him in a thick accent, that it was further along, and that Phil would have to cross into Frith Street.

A few minutes later found Phil Stone passing Meard Street, turning into a small street, towards the end of which he could see the sign of the Black Moth. He walked slowly along trying to make up his mind what sort of action he intended to take once he got inside the place. He glanced down at his ordinary dark suit, he knew from what Thelma had told him that Ray Mercury catered for a clientele prepared to spend more on one evening's entertainment than he would get in a whole month's pay-packet.

As if to emphasize his own circumstances, a huge, shining limousine purred past and stopped, and he saw two men in evening dress get out of the car and go into the club, the burly figure of the commissionaire saluting them deferentially. Here, he decided, was the first obstacle he had to surmount, this six-footer, broad-shouldered with a battered face, and small eyes under scarred, thickened eyebrows, the commissionaire. The man was an ex-prize-fighter, it was written all over him.

The piggy eyes under the knitted brows fastened on him as he approached, and he could feel the commissionaire appraising him for what he was worth, and Phil realized that he did not look the sort of person who would be welcomed warmly at the Black Moth.

'Good evening,' he said politely. The other made no reply, only stared at him non-committally as Phil went on: 'Mr. Mercury in the club to-night?'

'Why, do you want to see him?'

'That was the general idea,' Phil said.

'Does he know you?'

'Not yet.'

'Got an appointment?'

'Not exactly, but I thought that you and I might arrange that between us.'

Phil smiled and put his hand into his pocket, and drew out his note-case from which he pulled a ten-shilling note. The commissionaire's attitude relaxed, in fact it softened considerably, the piggy eyes became less suspicious.

'What do you want to see him about?'

'Just a little private matter.'

'You aren't a newspaper reporter or something?'

'No. I'm a friend of a friend of his.'

'What's the name of the friend?'

'One of the girls working here.'

'What girl?'

Still holding the ten-shilling note out, Phil Stone hesitated for a moment. Since he didn't know the names of any of the other girls, he decided it was not any use trying to bluff. 'Her name's Thelma Grayson,' he said.

The other considered this for a moment and then extended a thick hand. The stubby fingers closed over the ten shillings and transferred it to his hip-pocket.

'Okay,' he said, 'nip in. Ask one of the waiters if Mr. Mercury is downstairs, or if he is up in his office at the back of the Club.'

Phil grinned at him conspiratorially and went into the foyer; he could hear the sound of quiet dance-music beyond glass swing-doors, but he turned towards a short flight of thickly-carpeted stairs on his left. A waiter's back was ahead of him and as the black-coated figure disappeared through the door and with a glance at the commissionaire, who was busily engaged in looking the other way, Phil went quickly and silently up the stairs.

Ray Mercury might be either downstairs or up in his private office, might he? Come to think of it, Phil thought that the quiet of his office, away from the sound of dance-music, hurrying waiters and people out for an evening's entertainment, would be more suitable for what he had in mind. As he went on up, the curving staircase softly lit by bracketed lights on the walls, Phil turned over in his mind what precisely he was going to say to Ray Mercury. Should he hurl abuse at him, challenge him to settle it with bare fists there and then; or should he remain calm and cool, take it easy? But in that case, what would be the object of this call he was making? Mingled with these questions was the thought that the girl he loved had worked and danced here, at the Black Moth, and that the man he was about to confront face-to-face was the man who had brought about her death.

Now he had gained the top of the stairs and ahead of him was a softly-lit passage, with a thick carpet, and two doors, one on either side, and at the end a third door. Phil remembered the commissionaire saying that Ray Mercury's office was the one at the back of the club, and his sense of direction told him that the door at the end was the one he was looking for.

The dance-music was faint and distant as he approached the door. He turned the crystal door-handle and went in. The aroma of cigar-smoke and perfume greeted him, and then he noticed a sharper odour that seemed to sting his nostrils. He stood on the threshold as if carved out of rock. There before him, in the softly-lit room with its air of luxury, sprawled beside the ornate gleaming desk on his back, lay the figure who he had last seen in the witness-box in the Coroner's Court at Hatford. It was Ray Mercury.

Hesitantly he stepped forward and stood staring down at the inert figure. He saw the dark patch on the immaculate shirt-front and he bent and put his hand just above the dark patch, over the heart. Phil knew that the man was dead. He stood up, his mind a turmoil of conflicting emotions and questions. As he straightened himself he saw a note on the flat top of the desk. He was about to reach for it when there was a movement behind him and he heard a voice saying:

'What is wrong —?'

Phil saw that it was a waiter who had come into the office. He spoke warily, with a strong Italian accent. He was a short, dark-haired, pudgy man. He was looking at the sprawling figure and broke into a stream of excited Italian. As he finished whatever it was he was saying he, too, knelt beside the body, and then looked up at Phil Stone.

'Who did this?'

'How the hell should I know,' Phil said. 'I came in here a moment ago and there he was.'

The waiter squinted at him, his dark eyes suspicious, then he straightened himself and leaning across the desk, grabbed a telephone.

'What are you going to do?' Phil asked.

'Phone for a doctor.'

'It's not a doctor you want,' Phil said with grim humour, 'it's more like an undertaker.'

The other flashed a long look at him. He hesitated and as if he had experienced a sudden brainwave, he put down the telephone.

'I don't have to phone,' he said, 'there's a doctor here already.'

'Oh?' Phil said.

'Yes,' the other said, 'Dr. Morelle. He's having supper downstairs.'

Chapter Eleven

Dr. Morelle took a long drag at his inevitable Le Sphinx, and idly observed the man in the brilliant spotlight. The man was wearing sleek evening-tails, with a rather exaggerated white tie. He was pale-faced and his hair gleamed a grey, silvery colour, brushed back from a centre-parting.

He was approaching the climax of his act, which had been a fascinating display of conjuring dexterity with a pack of playing-cards. Now as his audience watched he was causing a card to rise from the bouquet of flowers he was holding in one hand into his other hand which he held two feet or more above. It was a card which he had previously asked a red-haired woman with a gay party sitting at a ringside table to select and without telling what the card was, return it to the pack he had held before her. Now, the card was held high in the conjurer's fingers and a burst of applause greeted the red-head's smiling acknowledgment that it was her own chosen card.

'I know how he got her to choose that particular card,' Inspector Hood said to Dr. Morelle from the corner of his mouth. 'All he did was to cut the pack in two so that when he puts the pack together again he returned the top half underneath the original lower half. The card which she'd picked out and then returned on top of the lower half is now on top of the pack. That way he only has to remember where the card was returned to the pack, he doesn't have to know what it was. Simple.'

Dr. Morelle nodded with a thin smile.

'But what I don't get,' Inspector Hood said with a frown, 'is how the devil he makes the card rise up in the air like that from that bunch of flowers?'

Dr. Morelle's smile became a trifle condescending. 'The devil has nothing to do with it,' he said, through a cloud of cigarette-smoke. 'The secret lies in a black thread, one end of which he attaches to the card, and which passes through a tiny eyelet on that ring he is wearing on his right finger to a tiny spring drum which is concealed up his coat-sleeve. To manipulate the card by this means is child's play.'

Inspector Hood looked at Dr. Morelle admiringly. 'Is there any mystery on this earth that your mind can't unravel?' he said.

Dr. Morelle contrived to smile deprecatingly. 'You flatter me,' he said. 'My thought processes would be slow indeed if they remained baffled for long by anything our friend out there,' he nodded in the direction of the bowing smiling conjurer, 'could think up.'

Inspector Hood glanced at him quickly. 'I didn't know you too knew him,' he said.

'I did,' Dr. Morelle said, 'only not under the name he is performing under.'

'Aces La Rue,' the other said. 'Trust him to think up one like that, it's quite a handle.'

Detective-Inspector Hood of Scotland Yard was a square-faced, burly man, who looked a trifle out of place in the sophisticated surroundings of the Black Moth. He and Dr. Morelle occupied a table tucked away in a corner, but with a clear view of the dance floor. The orchestra had been playing softly during Aces La Rue's act, now as the conjurer was making his final bow the music reached a crescendo. Inspector Hood glanced round at the faces of the women, their jewels glittering in the reflection of the spotlight's glare and at the gleaming white of the men's shirt-fronts. He turned his head as Dr. Morelle said:

'I am very grateful to you for inviting me along, and it's a pity that Miss Frayle could not accompany me. But there is a great deal of work to be done, so I left her busy at Harley Street. I've no doubt she fears,' he went on, 'that without her guidance I shall come to some wicked end, though since she knows that I am with you, perhaps she may feel less cause for concern.'

Inspector Hood chuckled. 'I'm sorry she couldn't have made it,' he said. 'I am sure Miss Frayle would have had a good time.'

Neither he, still less Dr. Morelle, had shown any interest in the first item of the evening's entertainment, a line of scantily-dressed girls going through their dance routine, it was not until Aces La Rue's appearance that Hood had sat up and taken some notice, and had watched his act attentively. Now the conjurer had made his exit and the line of girls were out again, wearing as little as before, though this time their heads were adorned with head-dresses of multi-coloured feathers, which bobbed up and down during the energetic dance that followed.

'At any rate it was gratifying to learn,' Dr. Morelle was saying, 'that he is now treading a straighter and narrower path than he has in the past.'

The last time Dr. Morelle had met the individual who called himself Aces La Rue had been on a liner London-bound from New York. Then the conjurer had been working the Atlantic run as a professional card-sharper. One night two young men whom he had attempted to mulct, taking a poor view of his activities had inveigled him to a deserted part of the deck, and proceeded to beat him up. It chanced that Dr. Morelle had come along in time to scare the two men off, and to attend to the card-sharper, who was in a pretty sorry state as a result of the going-over he had suffered.

From that moment the latter had sworn his undying gratitude to Dr. Morelle, who had in turn suggested to him that he might turn his undoubted talents as a card-manipulator to a more honest purpose. Not that Dr. Morelle, whose knowledge of the criminal mind was deep and wide, had felt particularly confident that his advice would prove acceptable. But it would seem that his pessimism in this respect had proved unjustified. The card-sharper had turned over a new leaf and adopting a new name was apparently employing his skill legitimately.

Dr. Morelle was at the Black Moth that night on Inspector Hood's invitation, the latter explaining to him that he himself was invited along by someone he'd known as a criminal and whom he'd had the job of arresting two or three times in the past, but who had abandoned a career of crime to become a performer on the music-halls and in cabaret.

When Hood mentioned the name of the man, Aces La Rue, who wanted to prove to the detective that he was no longer a crook, and to exhibit his prowess as a member of the entertainment profession, it had conveyed nothing to Dr. Morelle. Dr. Morelle had accepted his old friend's invitation not with alacrity, or pleasurable anticipation. Night-clubs were not in Dr. Morelle's line. But Hood had been so insistent and persuasive that in the end he had agreed to join him.

So it was with some amusement tinged with a sense of self-satisfaction that he had recognized the man who was the main reason for the detective-inspector's presence as none other than the card-sharper who, by his intervention that night on board the Southampton-bound liner, he felt he had first set on the road away from crime.

He was wondering whether La Rue had observed him sitting with Inspector Hood, and if so what his reaction had been. And he was deciding that his presence might have passed unnoticed by the conjurer since Hood had chosen a table inconspicuously in the shadows of a corner, when a voice said deferentially in his ear:

'Dr. Morelle.'

It was a waiter who was hovering behind him, his voice calm, but there was an agitated expression in his eyes. Dr. Morelle gave him a questioning glance and the other stepped closer.

'Could you come, Dr. Morelle, please? There's been a slight — er — accident.'

Dr. Morelle observed that the dark-haired man with his marked Italian accent was perspiring round his pudgy jowls, and he turned to Inspector Hood with a quizzical expression.

'A doctor's work is never done,' Inspector Hood said, with a little chuckle as Dr. Morelle rose to his feet. The waiter hesitated and looked tentatively at the detective. Dr. Morelle caught his glance.

'Would you like him to come too?' he said. 'This is Detective-Inspector Hood of Scotland Yard.'

The other gasped, then mopped his face with a handkerchief. 'Perhaps you would, sir?' he said to Hood. 'I am afraid something — er — something unpleasant has happened.

Dr. Morelle and the Inspector exchanged glances and followed the waiter round the back of the tables at which the night-club patrons sat watching the line of girls, through the swing-doors, and up the thick-carpeted stairs to Ray Mercury's office.

On the way the waiter told them in his voluble broken English what he had found when he entered the office, and how he earlier had recognized Dr. Morelle from a newspaper photograph he had seen several weeks before.

Inspector Hood made no comment as they hurried along the softly-lit passage at the head of the stairs, only a muttered grunt of surprise when he realized that it was the boss of the Black Moth Club who was lying dead in his office.

The office-door was open and Dr. Morelle led the way, followed by Hood, the waiter puffing behind, still chattering.

Phil Stone stood between the sprawled figure on the floor and the wide desk. He made no move, said nothing to Dr. Morelle as he knelt beside the body.

Dr. Morelle's gaze flickered over him, and then it took in the note on the desk. Inspector Hood saw it at the same moment, and his large hand poised

69

over it for a moment, then reached for the telephone instead. He was about to lift the receiver when he glanced at the waiter.

'You said you picked it up before you remembered Dr. Morelle was here?'

The waiter nodded, the detective muttered something to himself, then picked up the phone. As he dialled and waited for a reply, he looked questioningly at Dr. Morelle who glanced up at him with one eyebrow raised significantly.

'Dead?'

Dr. Morelle nodded. 'Shot through the heart. No doubt the bullet's from the pistol under the desk where it's fallen.'

Dr. Morelle heard an exclamation from Phil Stone as the latter moved forward to see a small, gleaming black automatic which lay just out of sight under the desk about a foot from the dead man's outstretched right hand.

Hood gave a quick nod, and then spoke briefly into the receiver, giving instructions. He hung up and then he picked up the note, and while he was squinting at it he muttered to Dr. Morelle. 'Curious,' he said, 'they usually go in for blowing the brains out.'

Dr. Morelle glanced at the crimson patch on the dead man's shirt front, then he looked round the luxuriously furnished office, his gaze lighting on the waiter, who stood anxiously in the background, before it rested once more on Phil Stone. His eyes held him for a moment, then they returned to Inspector Hood.

'He appears to have had all the material necessities for a quiet, untroubled life,' he said.

'This note seems to give the idea,' Inspector Hood said, and he read it aloud: 'I can't get poor Julie Grayson out of my mind. I know some people say I am responsible for her death. So I am taking this way out. All my love to you, darling Greta. Ray.'

Dr. Morelle raised an eyebrow. 'Julie Grayson?' he said musingly, and moved closer to Inspector Hood to read the note over the other's thick, heavy shoulder.

'An inquest a day or two ago, I seem to recall,' Dr. Morelle said. 'Verdict of suicide was returned against a girl who was employed here. And this man,' he indicated the body of Ray Mercury, 'gave evidence to the effect that she was infatuated with him, and committed suicide on account of it.'

'That's it. He drove her to her death.'

Dr. Morelle and the detective-inspector turned round to Phil Stone, his face was contorted as he was about to continue, but Inspector Hood interrupted him.

'I was about to ask you one or two questions,' he said to him drily.

'You don't need to ask me anything,' Phil replied. 'I can tell you everything that happened.'

'Suppose you tell us who you are for a start?'

'My name is Stone. I'm a ship's officer, I arrived back in England only a few days ago.'

Dr. Morelle had already noticed the sunburn on the young man's face which did not fit in with the tired shadows beneath his blue eyes.

'I came up to his office,' Phil Stone went on, 'opened the door, and there he was.'

Inspector Hood turned to glance at the waiter. 'That's what you were telling us,' he said 'he told you, when he came up here.'

The waiter nodded, and mopped his glistening brow with his handkerchief again.

'It's true enough,' Phil said. 'I admit I came up here with the intention of causing trouble. I was prepared to give Ray Mercury a beating-up. But when I came in the room the job had been done for me.'

'You would hardly describe yourself as being depressed by your discovery?' Dr. Morelle said quietly.

'Who are you anyway?'

'I am afraid I forgot to make the introductions,' Hood said. 'This is Dr. Morelle, and I'm Detective-Inspector Hood of Scotland Yard. He and I happened to be around having a quiet little meal when the waiter brought us up here. Other police-officers are on their way.'

'I can't say I'm sorry,' Phil Stone said to Dr. Morelle. 'Though I must admit he didn't strike me as the sort who'd take his own life.'

'People do funny things for funny reasons,' Inspector Hood said.

Dr. Morelle was wearing a thoughtful expression on his gaunt face. 'I seem to recall that it was you who first found the girl referred to in the note,' he said. 'The girl whose death you say this man caused?'

'Yes,' Phil said, 'I found her.'

Dr. Morelle noted the tension in his voice, the haunted look in his eyes, and he wondered what were the emotions and how deep ran the beat of human hearts that criss-crossed behind this strange story of two deaths so near to each other and concerning two people who were so well known to one another. The girl had been an unknown quantity, so far as the police were aware. A poor deluded creature who had apparently made a fool of herself over a man, and then had chosen a tragic way out. But from what Inspector Hood had mentioned to Dr. Morelle that evening concerning the owner of the Black Moth Club, the late Ray Mercury was not a particularly impressive specimen of humanity. His past was not the sort that would have stood a great deal of looking into, his photograph together with details of some of the more unsavoury episodes which had engaged his attention, and which had brought him to the notice of the police were to be found in the Criminal Record Office at Scotland Yard.

Dr. Morelle's cogitations were interrupted by Inspector Hood saying to the waiter: 'You or anybody hear the sound of a shot?'

'No, sir. I would not have known what happened if I had not come up here already because I wished to speak to Mr. Mercury about one or two business-matters. But it is not really surprising,' the waiter went on, 'that nothing was heard. The walls and door are sound-proofed. It is almost impossible, unless you are close outside the door, to hear anything in here.'

'Mr. Mercury liked to be quiet when he was in his office?' the Scotland Yard man said.

'That is right, sir.'

The door opened wide, and Inspector Hood, without turning his head, was about to announce the police had arrived when a voice stopped him.

'Dr. Morelle,' the newcomer said, 'at last I've found you.'

It was Miss Frayle who stood on the threshold.

Dr. Morelle spun round slowly to observe her with a frosty smile. Miss Frayle came forward tentatively, blinking a little behind her horn-rimmed glasses.

'I'd finished my work,' she said, 'and you were still not back, so I thought I'd come along and find you, you know you have a long day to-morrow. They said downstairs that you were —'

Miss Frayle broke off with a horrified gasp as her eyes encountered the figure on the floor. Inspector Hood made a move towards her as if to mask the body, but he was too late to hide that inert shape.

'Is — is he dead?' Miss Frayle said.

'If he isn't,' Dr. Morelle said, 'he's giving a remarkably good imitation.'

Chapter Twelve

Aces La Rue sprawled on his bed in his two-room flat overlooking a corner of Old Compton Street. Through the open window came the daytime noises of Soho's busy streets below. Aces had just returned from buying the day's groceries. From where he lay he could see through the open door his string shopping-bag bulging over on his sitting-room table. There was nothing else to the flat except a cubby-hole out on the landing, with a gas-stove and a sink and a few shelves, and a bathroom upstairs, which was shared by tenants of the flat above.

The place suited Aces. He liked to have a dump right in the heart of London, in the centre of things, among the teeming streets he knew so well, close to the theatres and clubs and night-cellars and dives; and it was nice when he was playing dates in the provinces to know it was waiting for him when he came back.

Sometimes he had to admit to himself it looked a crummy joint, but it suited him. Of course, there were times when he considered that the activities of the tenants who occupied rooms on the two floors beneath his rather lowered the tone of the place: the sound of clumping feet on the bare stair-boards which ran up from the street-entrance beside the Continental provisions store was sometimes a source of considerable irritation.

However, live and let live had always been Aces' motto, and as long as people let him alone, he was prepared to let them get along with their business. He wanted no part of anybody else's business. He was strictly on his ownsome.

Yawning loudly, it had been a very late night with that funny business at the Black Moth, Aces rose and strolled to the window. The usual swarm of cars, swerving taxis, and people. The smell of coffee and cooking from nearby cafés and restaurants drifted up to him with the odour of petrol on the warm air. The usual gossiping group of men of various nationalities, creeds and colours, in their gaudy suits and ties, hanging about, gossiping about every subject under the sun, from girls to the racing-form.

Aces' mind switched back to last night at the Black Moth. For a moment, Aces sweated gently, he didn't like that sort of thing going on around him.

People letting guns off and killing themselves, it made him feel uncomfortable. Death was pretty inevitable anyway, he couldn't understand why people wanted to take a short cut to it.

Funny coincidence, he mused, it happening the very same night when old Inspector Hood had looked in, and brought Dr. Morelle with him, too. Though Mercury's suicide had taken the attention off his performance and their interest in him, and he hadn't had a chance of a word with either of them afterwards. He wondered if Dr. Morelle, who must have recognized him, of course, had mentioned that business on board the liner to the Scotland Yard man. Aces decided that he hadn't, that Dr. Morelle wasn't the sort to open his trap about something like that.

Aces was a respectable citizen now, engaged in a legitimate profession for whatever fee he, or his agent, could screw out of who booked the act. Come to think of it, he'd have to look for a new spot in London now that Mercury was a goner, the club was certain to be closed for a spell, longer than he could afford to be out of work.

He saw the groups shifting below as a newspaper-van dropped off a bundle of the early edition of the evening papers to the old chap who sold them on the corner.

There would be something about Ray Mercury, Aces thought.

He went out of the flat, down the bare stairs, and out into the street. He was back in his sitting-room within a few minutes, sitting smoking a cheap cheroot and reading the story on the front page.

Ray Mercury had made the front page this time, all right. Aces had read a stop press reference in his morning paper to the happenings at the Black Moth; now, here was a couple of columns devoted to the night-club owner's death.

'SOHO NIGHT-CLUB DEATH,' the headlines ran. 'Ray Mercury, owner of the Black Moth, well-known night-club, died in the early hours of this morning while the band played and the patrons danced, joked and drank their champagne. He had been shot dead, a pistol was found in his hand. The police have taken possession of a note in the dead man's handwriting, they say there appears to be no evidence of foul play.'

Aces took a deep drag at his cheroot and then read on: 'Ray Mercury recently gave evidence at the inquest on Julie Grayson, a former dancer at his club. According to the verdict at the inquest she had committed suicide.'

Reading between the lines, Aces decided, it looks like they're linking the two things. 'It was revealed at the inquest on Julie Grayson,' he read, 'that she had been in love with Mercury and that he had broken off their association.'

Aces put the paper down, staring through the window at the upper floors of the houses across the street. It looked like Ray Mercury was upset about the girl, it had preyed on his mind, so he had gone and shot himself, that was what the paper was making it look like. Only the thing was, he thought, the idea of Ray Mercury shooting himself over a girl was a bit out of character. He didn't know him well, he'd played at his club for about four months, and hardly ever met him around, but he'd heard tales about Ray Mercury. Not particularly nice stories. And then wasn't there some beautiful blonde who was his wife in the background? A foreign piece, people said, who no one saw at the club.

Aces La Rue shrugged to himself. How could you tell what people in Ray Mercury's racket would do next? He could be half-filled with dope at the time, or ginned up to the ears. You couldn't tell with people like that. They were a nutty crowd and no mistake. He recalled that henchman of his, Luke Roper, he called himself. He looked as if he was a dope-addict, if anyone did.

'Always give me the creeps, he did,' Aces said to himself. He had long got into the habit of talking to himself. 'I'd sooner shake hands with a snake than with Luke.'

He threw his paper on a rickety chair and glanced at his wrist-watch on its imitation gold bracelet. Time he took a stroll down Charing Cross Road and met a few music-hall pals, listened to show-business gossip and looked in on his agent, to remind him Aces La Rue was now swelling the ranks of the unemployed.

He went into the kitchen with the object of making himself a cup of coffee, in order to buck up his spirits preparatory to going out, when he heard a knock on the door of the flat.

Aces began to sweat. Don't tell me it's the cops, he thought, wanting to ask him questions about last night's goings-on. He didn't like the idea of that at all. He had nothing to fear from a visit from the gendarmes, he had nothing on his conscience, but the idea of meeting the cops just made him sweat, that was all.

'Can't be a flattie,' he muttered to himself. 'I'd have heard his big boots clumping up the stairs. I'll go.'

He went and opened the door.

The woman who stood there, hesitantly, was deathly pale and Aces was shocked by the haunted stare in her long grey eyes. He saw that she clutched a crumpled newspaper.

'Why, Thelma,' he said. 'This is a surprise, and a pleasant surprise at that.'

He held the door open for her. She didn't smile as he took her hand, and he found it cold and unresponsive.

'I hoped you'd be here,' she said. She spoke as if she was shivering. 'I'm so glad.'

'You wanted to see me?' Aces' expression was baffled. 'That's fine,' he said. 'Fine. Come on in and park your chassis.'

To Thelma, as she sat in a sagging arm-chair, it was as if she had come to this place instinctively. Her mind a maelstrom, all she knew was that she must seek help and this strange little grey-haired man, it seemed to her, was her only hope, there was no one else she could turn to.

Since she had left the Black Moth there had been no sleep for her. Time had meant nothing. Where she had wandered, where she had sat, brooding alone in all-night cafés, she could not have remembered, before eventually she had returned to the Charlotte Street flat. The past hours had been like a nightmare, pacing up and down her flat through the grey dawn, racked and tormented by the enormity of the thing she had done, she had at last forced her will to take command of her shattered nerves. She had begun to think and reason coldly. She had left the flat again to walk and try and reach a decision, to find an answer to the dread question: what should she, a murderess do, with her life now?

Then, an hour ago, she had bought an early edition of an evening newspaper and experienced a shock that had numbed every fibre of her being.

She assented automatically when Aces asked her to have a cup of coffee with him, and he had started to bustle around the kitchen.

'This is great seeing you again, Thelma,' he called through the open door. 'Though I'm not used to entertaining classy dames like you, so you must excuse this little nest of mine, I'm afraid the joint is a bit of a shambles.'

While he busied himself preparing the coffee, he contrived to study the girl covertly. A skilled student of human nature, he tried to guess at the state of mind of his visitor. Was she still, he wondered, grieving over the death of her sister? A darned shame about that kid. He'd liked both of them when he had got to know them at the club.

'You said you wanted to see me,' he said, at last, as she took a cup of coffee from him. 'If there's any way I can help?'

She looked at him with strange intentness. A sense of uneasiness filled him, a feeling of disquiet. Something was going to break, he thought, that he wasn't going to want much of a part of. He sighed inwardly. He wished she'd taken whatever it was on her mind to unload somewhere else.

'You may not want to help me,' she said, 'when I tell you what it is.'

'We'll cross that bridge when we come to it,' he said. 'Just go ahead and make with the talk.'

She leaned forward, watching him, her face pale and drawn.

'Would you help me,' she asked, 'even if you knew I'd killed someone?'

Aces' jaw dropped as he stared at the girl. Then he forced a sympathetic expression to his face. 'You mean you ran over someone in a car?' he said.

'I've killed a man,' she said, her voice low and harsh. 'Murdered him.'

'You — you murdered a man?' He chuckled shakily. 'You kidding?'

'This is no joke. I'm deadly serious and I'm frightened, but I killed him.'

'You've been letting things get on top of you,' Aces said. 'It's the shock of your sister's death, poor kid. Delayed shock that's what. Now you just get these ideas out of your head. You need to relax, take things easy for a while.'

'I must tell you,' she said. 'I must tell somebody. I shot Ray Mercury.'

He lowered the cheroot he had just lit and was about to take a pull at. 'Now I know you're living in some kind of nightmare,' he said. 'Why, I was just reading the paper. It practically says he committed suicide.'

'I went there last night,' she said, then she opened the newspaper with trembling hands and showed him the story similar to the one he had already read for himself in his paper. 'That's what I can't understand. I know I was there. I fired at him and saw him fall — and yet this morning I bought this paper, and they say he was found lying with a gun in his hand. I don't know what's happened. You must help me. Tell me what to do. I'm going crazy thinking of it.'

'You'll have to let this sink in,' Aces said. Privately, he was concluding that the tragedy of her sister's death followed by this shock of Ray Mercury had been too much for her. 'You really believe what you're telling me?'

'I tell you,' Thelma Grayson said passionately, 'I meant to kill him for what he did to Julie.'

'You'd better go through this right from the start,' Aces said, thinking that he might as well let her rattle away at him if it would do her any good. He'd got time to spare anyway, and she was a nice-looking girl and sweet all right, and he liked her and he'd liked her poor kid of a sister.

'I couldn't bottle it up any longer,' she said, her voice throaty and low-toned. 'I had to tell somebody and ask their help.'

Yes, he was the only one she could come to in her hours of anguish. She had thought of telling Phil Stone everything, once or twice at her flat she had picked up the telephone to speak to him. But she had been afraid that he would not understand, she was afraid, she had admitted to herself, that he would say she should go to the police. She wanted to hear something different, in her agony of mind she wanted to hear that there was an easy way out, a simple way.

And then she had read in the newspaper story the reference to the young man, Phil Stone, who had discovered Ray Mercury dead, and she had guessed that he had gone to see the man who had been responsible for the death of the girl he loved, no doubt to tell him what he thought of him, to thrash him with his bare hands. It was like Phil to have planned to do just that.

So she had kept away from him, she had, at last, come to Aces La Rue, with his worldly-wide experience, for help.

'You see,' she said to him, 'this newspaper story has altered everything. If he committed suicide, then I didn't murder him, after all. It's all so strange, and mad — and yet I know I was there, and I did shoot him . . .'

She paused to gulp down some coffee from a cup that trembled in her hand. Then she spoke slowly, and carefully, with cold emphasis.

'I went there late last night,' she said. 'I don't know the exact time. Nobody saw me. I got a key to the door at the back of the place a week or two ago. It was lost by the commissionaire and I happened to find it, and, I don't know why, I hung onto it. There was nobody about. I found him alone in his office, and there was only one thing I wanted to do. It had been in my mind all the time since Julie died.'

Aces took a drag at his cheroot, but it was cold in his mouth. He was staring at her, incredulity slowly receding from his face, as she went on, her eyes wide and staring as she pictured the grim scene.

78

'He began to get frightened,' she said, her voice dropping to a whisper. 'As he stood up behind his desk I fired at him, and fell forwards across the desk. I went out, still no one saw me. Afterwards I was panic-stricken, horrified at what I had done.'

There was a few moments' silence. Aces pushed a hand through his silver-grey hair. Then he said: 'Far as I can see I'd forget the whole thing. You'll only lay up trouble for yourself if you start talking now. The police seem to think by what the papers say, that it's an open and closed case. So why not let sleeping dogs lie, why stir up trouble for yourself?'

'But don't you see,' she said desperately. 'It'll be preying on my mind forever if I thought I really had killed him. If this is right, and he committed suicide, then I didn't murder him, I couldn't have done. It's all so crazy and mixed up — but if I can only find out the truth.'

'I get it, I get it all,' Aces said, sorry for the girl, yet wishing fervently she hadn't pushed this problem on him. 'According to you, you left him for dead, then he gets up and shoots himself.' He thought for a moment, eyeing her. 'Where did you get the gun?'

'I borrowed it. From someone I know.'

'What did you do with it afterwards?'

'I just put it in my coat-pocket.'

'You still got it?'

She shook her head. 'I threw it away,' she said. 'I can't remember where exactly. I was so muddled in my head. But I threw it into some rubbish dump, on a bombsite, somewhere. I just threw it away.'

'I see,' he said. Then he shrugged. 'I don't suppose it makes any difference. If it turns up no one need trace it to you or what happened at the club. And it may never turn up at that.' He broke off. 'But why did you think I could straighten this out for you?'

She looked at him appealingly. 'Julie and I always liked you, we always felt you'd been around, you knew the world. I thought you might know about these things, the way the police work on a case like this. I'm sorry to have loaded my trouble on you, but —'

'I don't want to get mixed up with the police, and that's flat,' Aces said. 'Already, if what you've told me is true, I'm an accessory after the fact.' He shifted uncomfortably and re-lit the cold cheroot.

'I'd no idea of getting you in trouble,' Thelma Grayson said. 'And if you feel you ought to go to them —'

'Give away a pal?' he said, grinning at her. 'Not likely. I'll keep my trap shut. And you should do the same. That's my advice to you, Thelma. Let it blow over.'

'I can't,' she said, quietly. 'If I can't find out, I'm afraid I'll have to go to the police in the end. I just don't know what to do, what to think. I'm scared and yet I want to know the worst.'

Aces got up and paced the room. 'I want to help you.' He stopped pacing suddenly, a gleam in his narrowed eyes. 'I've got it, I've got an idea. There's someone who can help you, who'll give you the best advice available.'

She stared at him eagerly. He swung round to her. She stood up and moved towards him.

'He was a good friend to me once,' he said. 'Come to think of it,' he added, a note of excitement creeping into his voice, 'he was there last night. Dr. Morelle, you go and see him. He lives in Harley Street.'

'Dr. Morelle?' she said.

He nodded and took her hands in his. They were still ice-cold and trembling. 'Listen, Thelma, he's the one man in the world who can fix this for you. Tell him I sent you, if you like, though I don't want to get mixed up too much in this. But tell Dr. Morelle what you've told me and leave the rest to him.'

Chapter Thirteen

Thelma Grayson flipped through the pages of the Medical Directory for the current year, until she came to what she wanted to read: MORELLE, she read, 221B. Harley Street, W.1 (Tel. Langham 05011) — M.D. Berne (Univ. Berne Prize & Gold Medallist) 1942: F.R.C.P. Lond. 1932 (Univ. Vienna, Salzburg, Carfax, U.S.A.); Phys. Dept. Nerv. Dis. & Lect. in Neurol. Rome Academy, 1929; Lect. & Research Fell. Sorbonne, 1928; Carfax, U.S.A. Fell. Med. Research Council 1930; Research Fell., Salzburg Hosp. 1931; Pathol. Rudolfa Clin. Berne; Medico-Psychol. Trafalgar Hosp. & Clin. Lond; Hon. Cons. Psychiat. Welbeck Hosp. Lond. Author 'Psychol. aspects of prevent, treat. of drug addiction,' Amer. Med. Wkly., 1932; 'Study of analysis in ment. treat.,' Ib., 1930; 'Nervous and mental aspect of drug addict,' Jl. of Res. in Psychopathol, 1931; 'Hypnot. treat. in nerve & ment. disorder,' Amer. Med. Jnl., 1930; and a list of further publications up to the current year on similar themes; etc., etc.

She got up from the table in the public library near Leicester Square, where she had found herself after leaving Aces La Rue, and returned the directory to its place, and took up Who's Who for the current year. She read Dr. Morelle's Christian names, but there was no date, place or details of his birth given. Educated: Sorbonne, Rome, Vienna, she read. M.D. Berne, 1923 (for further details of career as medical practitioner see Medical Directory — current year): Lecturer on medico-psychological aspects of criminology to New York Police Bureau, 1934; Lecturer and medico-psychiat. to police bureaux and criminological authorities of Geneva, Rome, Milan and Paris, 1935–1937. Published miscellaneous papers on medical and scientific subjects (see Medical Directory — current year). Writings for journals include: 'Auguste Dupin versus Sherlock Holmes — A Study in Ratiocination,' London Archive & Atlantic Weekly, 1931; 'The Criminal versus Society,' English Note-book, Le Temps Moderne & New York Letter, 1933; and further publications on allied subjects up to the current year; etc., etc. Address: 221B Harley Street, London, W.1. Recreations: Criminology and fencing. European fencing champion (Epee) Switzerland, 1927–28–29. Clubs: None.

Returning thoughtfully to the flat in Charlotte Street, Thelma Grayson remembered a glossy magazine she had once read which carried an article about Dr. Morelle. She found the magazine, it was a year old, and turned the pages, until she came to the article again.

'Not to have compiled a case-book would have been unusual in any practising medical man,' Thelma read, 'the recording of particulars relative to his patients being a mere matter of routine. When one regards Dr. Morelle as somewhat above the average physician, the inclination is to expect that during such a wide and singularly varied career he must have compiled fairly extensive case-books and of more than ordinary interest.

'In fact his case-histories run into several volumes. In them is recorded in his characteristically neat and meticulous handwriting the minute and precise details of every case with which he has been associated.

'To say they make an intriguing contribution to the study of human nature could hardly be described as an overstatement. From the moment he began his career as a medical practitioner, Dr. Morelle has concerned himself only with the unusual, the bizarre. In these pages are crystallized all the frailties and foibles, the ever-insoluble mystery of the human mind and soul. Each case it seems adds yet another chapter to the remarkable history of human, inhuman or subhuman conduct. Therein is set down the illuminating if somewhat disturbing glimpses into such subterranean twistings of the brain, such tortuous writhings of the spirit as pass belief.

'Professional ethics apart Dr. Morelle has, of course, no desire that his memoirs shall remain other than secret. They are recorded purely for the study of medical colleagues, other men of science and anthropologists, to whom, as he is far from unaware, they are of inestimable value. There are other reasons besides why his memoirs may not be the subject of public scrutiny. In a number of cases those involved have been personages of importance, some of whom are still alive. In one or two instances political issues were involved, there were men in high places who entrusted Dr. Morelle with the safety of their honour and careers, so they might be disentangled from the sinister skeins in which they were caught. His integrity, they knew, was never in doubt.

'Again there are other cases whose publications to the world at large would bring distress to those persons still living who had been, indirectly or directly, implicated. And while Dr. Morelle's attitude towards his fellow-creatures is perhaps more accurately described as one of benign contempt, at no time has he sought deliberately to do harm to someone defenceless and unable to retaliate . . .'

At about this time the subject of the article Thelma Grayson was poring over was making his way along Chelsea Embankment, returning to Harley Street. Dr. Morelle had just enjoyed a cup of tea with Sir Burton Muir, the eminent Q.C., in his house overlooking the river. As he strolled along in the pale light of early evening, his sword-stick rapping sharply on the pavement, Dr. Morelle's mind went back to another occasion when he had walked back from Sir Burton's house, the occasion of his very first meeting with Miss Frayle.

It must have been all of four years ago, Dr. Morelle was deciding, and he could not repress a faint sigh at the way time went past. It seemed only yesterday, a late hour one moonless and rather misty night when he had been proceeding somewhat briskly along Chelsea Embankment. He had just left his old friend and a small party. It had been a pleasurable evening, good food excellently cooked and served, good wine; together with a flow of conversation befitting the intellect of Sir Burton and his guests, eminent in the fields of medicine and law. Dr. Morelle had as was his habit made brilliant contributions to each various topic of discussion, scoring points with his sardonic shafts of humour. He had left before the others, having in mind some work awaiting him unfinished in his laboratory at Harley Street. Now having decided to take a little exercise before ultimately hailing a taxi he was walking quickly along the Embankment in the direction of Chelsea Bridge.

Somewhere down-river a ship's siren had hooted mournfully and the Thames running past was dark and forbidding. The mist swirled chill and raw across the Embankment which seemed quite deserted. But as he strode on, his mind full of the research problems with which he presently proposed to grapple, Dr. Morelle passed a young woman leaning against the parapet. He might not have noticed her, so insignificant a figure she made, but something, a certain tenseness about her attitude caused him to throw her a passing glance.

A few paces on he paused to light a cigarette. As he flicked a flame against the tip of his Le Sphinx he glanced back, and snapping the cap of his lighter into place swiftly retraced his steps.

'You know,' he said to the young woman, and his tone was level and charged with a sardonic quirk, 'I don't think I should.'

She gave a startled gasp. His swift and noiseless approach had taken her utterly unawares. He regarded her. She was small and slim, pathetic in her shabby clothes, and she stared up at him wide-eyed through horn-rimmed spectacles which were perched awry on her nose. The look of desperation in her face gave way now to one of forlorn misery and wretchedness.

'Drowning's a cold and dismal affair only a fool would choose,' he said to her, his eyes glittering with inner amusement.

'I'm not going to —'

Her protest fading into a broken whisper, she turned away to stare down at the dark waters. Unmoved, he watched the tear-trickle run down her nose and splash onto the parapet. She said: 'Please — please leave me alone.'

He had no intention of acceding to her request until his curiosity had been satisfied. Insinuatingly he had said: 'Should I — er — call a policeman?'

Her face jerked up to him in terror. 'No. Oh, don't.'

'Very well. But in return you must tell me something. Who are you?'

She had answered him hesitantly: 'My name is Frayle — Miss Frayle.'

'And what, Miss Frayle,' and now he smiled thinly, 'apart from contemplating putting an end to your life, do you do?'

'I'm' — she corrected herself with a little shudder — 'I was a secretary-companion.'

'Your employer I presume having dispensed with your services?'

There had been a brief pause, and the reply was a whisper he had only just caught. 'She's dead.'

She began to dab her face with her handkerchief and blow her nose. Now she spoke hurriedly, blurting out the words as if anxious to get rid of them: 'I went out just now to post the letters — I do every evening — and when I came back I found her.'

He cut in quickly, deceptively soft-voiced. 'What happened then?'

'I — I lost my head. The way she looked. It was horrible.' She was shuddering violently, her face contorted at the remembered horror. 'I rushed from the flat.'

'Without waiting to call a doctor, or inform the police?'

'You don't understand. They'll say I did it — she was always telling people — her friends — that I hated her, I wanted to see her dead.' She broke off, adding pathetically: 'She wasn't very nice sometimes.'

'Supposing Miss Frayle,' he had said, 'you and I go back to the flat together?'

'I can't — I couldn't face it.'

He surveyed the glowing tip of his cigarette. Without looking at her, without raising his voice: 'I think it would be better for you if you did as I say.' And glancing at the mist swirling about them, he gave a somewhat over-elaborate shiver. 'Besides, I am finding it a little chilly.'

'I won't go back.' Her voice rose stubbornly. 'You can't make me.'

But, of course, she had been as wax in his hands. After all, Miss Frayle had told herself at the time, as she glanced up at his saturnine face shadowed by his soft black hat, he had said he was a doctor. Perhaps he really was. But with sinking heart she had been forced to admit he was like no other doctor she had ever met. Nothing kindly and gentle about him. This tall and gaunt, almost sinister figure with the sardonic smile and penetrating, mesmeric eyes.

Which was how Dr. Morelle had come to solve the mystery of the death of Miss Frayle's employer, and how Miss Frayle had found a new employer in Dr. Morelle. She had not remained in his employ ever since that fateful night of their first encounter. She had not found him easy exactly to get along with, nor had he found that she added up to the requirements he demanded for a secretary to the fullest extent. Far from it. But then Dr. Morelle's requirements were inclined to be somewhat exacting, and it was very doubtful if any human being existed who could have filled them.

And so Miss Frayle had a couple of times departed to other jobs, leaving Dr. Morelle in a state of mingled thankfulness and unease at what the future might hold for him in the shape of the next young woman to fill her place. In every case, though he would be the last to concede it, his most pessimistic apprehensions had been realized, and he had wished desperately that Miss Frayle, for all her flutterings and follies, her timorousness and her ingenuousness was back with him once more. Not that he would have admitted that to anyone, either. Certainly not to Miss Frayle, and hardly to himself.

And so this evening, as he paid off his taxi at the door of 221B Harley Street, he was filled with a sense of satisfaction that Miss Frayle was back with him once more. As he made his way to his study, where he knew she would be engaged upon some work for him, he decided that there was about her quite a quality of eagerness and refreshing enthusiasm, and that he must remember to resist those moments when she aroused him to bitter anger and sarcasm on account of some error of judgment she had committed, due merely to her excitably sanguine nature.

Miss Frayle was, in fact, bent over a batch of notes which she was filing, as he went into the study, and after idly watching her for a moment, he picked up the telephone and dialled.

'Hood,' he said presently, when the detective-inspector's voice answered him, 'Dr. Morelle speaking.'

'Inquest tomorrow, Doctor,' said Hood promptly. 'At Westminster Coroner's Court. I was about to ring you to ask you if you'd meet me there.'

'You will need formal evidence of my examination of the deceased?' Dr. Morelle said as he scribbled the time on his notepad. Then he went on: 'The p.m. reveal anything new?'

'We got the bullet out of him,' Hood said. 'Bernardelli .25, it was. Ballistics checked it was the same as the automatic found beside him. Only prints on the gun were Mercury's,' he added.

'Seems conclusive,' Dr. Morelle said thoughtfully. 'The note?'

There was a short pause, and then: 'His finger-prints were on it, as well as several others, including mine. Handwriting appears to be his. Let me put it to you this way,' Hood said. 'We're satisfied it's open-and-closed.'

Hanging-up, Dr. Morelle sat for a moment, finger-tips together, and deep in thought. He glanced at Miss Frayle.

'Did you form any opinion of the handwriting on Mercury's farewell-note?' he asked.

Miss Frayle did not look up from the work which was absorbing her attention. 'It was rather a scrawly sort of writing,' she said. 'And it looked rather shaky, as if he'd been in a hurry, I suppose.'

She broke off and looked at him as the front-doorbell rang. She eyed the clock on the writing-desk. It was a little late for consulting-hours, though, of course, Dr. Morelle's practice was not like that of the usual Harley Street physician. She had known the doorbell to ring announcing a caller for Dr. Morelle at an hour after midnight on more than one occasion. Even so, her pulse quickened with curiosity, as she hurried off to see who this caller might prove to be.

Dr. Morelle casually took a Le Sphinx from the human skull on his writing-desk which served somewhat ostentatiously as a cigarette-box, and lit it. Miss Frayle was back in a few moments, her eyes behind her horn-rims gleaming excitedly. She was evidently in a high state of excitement, and Dr. Morelle regarded her a trifle coldly.

'Do you know who it is? You'll never guess,' she said breathlessly.

'My dear Miss Frayle,' he said, through a cloud of cigarette smoke, 'how should I know if I know, when I haven't yet see our visitor?'

'But that's just it, Dr. Morelle, you have seen her. It's that young woman,' she said, 'the one we saw the other night, in the cemetery.'

Chapter Fourteen

In a swift glance Dr. Morelle had taken in his visitor's shadowed eyes, her pale face, with only a trace of makeup, and the way in which her hands clenched together convulsively as she sat down. 'You are the sister of the girl who died at Little Tiplow,' he said quietly. 'We have in fact seen each other before.' Her eyes were clouded, baffled pools. 'It was in the cemetery there,' Dr. Morelle said.

She stared at him, that recollection of the encounter night in the cemetery returned to her; she recalled the tall man and the fussy, smaller woman appearing out of the darkness as she was at Julie's graveside. She looked from Dr. Morelle to Miss Frayle: it was they who had been there, it was Dr. Morelle's torchlight which had been directed upon her. She murmured something about it being a strange coincidence.

Quickly Miss Frayle said something about it being a remarkable coincidence, that it was a small world, and then she went on to explain the reason for Dr. Morelle's and her presence in the cemetery. Dr. Morelle interrupted the glance Thelma Grayson was giving Miss Frayle.

'Anything you have to say to me can quite well be said in Miss Frayle's hearing,' he said quietly. 'It will be treated in the strictest confidence,' he smiled slightly, 'just imagine you are talking to your family doctor.'

'You may wish to — to — tell the police what I am going to tell you,' she said.

'Indeed?' Dr. Morelle was looking at her with composed interest, as if encouraging her to proceed with her story. Miss Frayle's pencil had dropped and rolled on the floor. Dr. Morelle glanced across at her sharply, and she blushed as she bent to pick it up.

'Before you give me the facts, Miss Grayson,' he said, 'perhaps you will tell me what made you decide to come to me?'

'I didn't know which way to turn,' Thelma Grayson burst out. 'I was at my wit's end,' she said. 'Then I remembered Aces La Rue. I knew him when my sister and I worked at the Black Moth.'

Her words came out in a rush.

'Aces La Rue,' Dr. Morelle said, an eyebrow raised at her quizzically.

'He does a card-act at the club,' she said. 'My sister and I were on friendly terms with him. We both thought he was so worldly-wise, so knowledgeable about life; and then when this terrible thing happened, and I was absolutely shocked and stunned, I remembered him.'

'He and I are not entirely unacquainted,' Dr. Morelle said, and he smiled reminiscently to himself.

'He told me you were the only person he could think of who might help me,' she said.

'I'm sure that was most flattering of him,' he said simply.

She hesitated, looking at him in almost agonized intensity. She gazed down at her hands, then glanced round the study, shadowy in the corners, and its walls book-lined. Then, at last, she turned to him again.

'Dr. Morelle, the newspapers are saying that Ray Mercury committed suicide last night in the Black Moth, but I know that it can't be true. It is impossible, because I went to the club last night, and shot him myself.'

As she uttered this rush of words, Miss Frayle was staring across at her, her eyes saucer-wide behind her horn-rimmed spectacles. Her mouth was open in astonishment, and her hands clutching at her notebook and pencil were shaking violently.

Dr. Morelle leaned back in his chair, clasping his hands together over his crossed legs. During the years he had heard many strange confessions in his shadowy study, but he could not recall a beautiful woman coming to him to tell him that a suicide was not a suicide at all, but a murder, and one she had herself perpetrated.

He studied Thelma Grayson through narrowed eyes. Her own gaze was fixed on his gaunt face. 'Let us be quite clear on one point, Miss Grayson,' he said. 'Do you mean this was,' he paused, 'some sort of an accident? That you and he struggled perhaps, and the gun went off?'

She said, almost in a whisper: 'I went there with the deliberate intention of killing him. I got this mad idea, which seized me like an obsession, so that I could think of nothing except revenge.'

'There are reasons,' Dr. Morelle said, 'into which I will not go now, which incline me to listen further to what you have to say. I have promised you that this is to be a strictly confidential interview, and so,' the faint smile he gave her had a curious warmth about it, it was a smile inviting her to reveal her closest secrets to him, and she took heart, 'continue with your story.'

Already some of the burden of anxiety and desperate panic seemed to slip from her. Her shoulders straightened, and her voice became stronger as she began talking quietly and calmly. She had taken all this time since she had left Aces La Rue to steel herself to force her footsteps in the direction of Harley Street. It had required all of her courage to ring the bell, all of her desperate determination not to run away.

'At the inquest the verdict was that she had committed suicide,' she was saying. 'But Julie had been driven to it. By him, as surely as if he had killed her himself.'

Dr. Morelle nodded. 'I read the newspaper story,' he said quietly.

She made a vague gesture. 'It is difficult to explain about him, but he had a sort of power over women. He smoothed his way into Julie's heart. She fell for it, she believed him, she was completely infatuated with him, nothing I said made any difference to her. She wouldn't listen to me. As the elder sister I'd always tried to look after her. But with him I was helpless. Until, one night, she came home utterly shaken and silent. At last he had come out into the open. He'd put on his true colours. I never knew what happened. We agreed that she should go down to Little Tiplow to our cottage there, and she would get him out of her mind. That was the last I saw of her alive.'

'So far as you knew,' Dr. Morelle said, 'she had made up her mind this man was no good for her, and meant to forget him and start afresh?'

'I was certain of it,' she said. Her voice hardened. 'Then, after the inquest, I was beginning to form the idea I had of settling with him.'

Dr. Morelle stirred in his chair. Miss Frayle was silent, her eyes on Thelma Grayson, full of pity for her. She shuddered at the thought that this girl had been driven by such emotional stress and desperate agony of mind that she had killed a man. The shadows had deepened in the corners of the study, Dr. Morelle sat outside the pool of light from the desk lamp, his dark eyes luminous under his knitted brows, the gaunt lines of his face set as if in ivory.

'I knew he would be in his office at that time,' Thelma Grayson said, more steadily now. 'I went in and faced him, and told him what I was going to do, and why. He was frightened, and tried to come round the desk to me,' she paused, 'and I fired. He fell across the desk, sprawling.'

'After you shot him,' Dr. Morelle said, 'and he fell forward, across the desk, did you touch him?'

Ernest Dudley

The other gave a grimace of horror. 'No, I saw what I had done, and remember putting the gun in my pocket, and I went out. I hardly knew where I was going.' She went on to describe how she had thrown the gun away.

'Can you give me any description of the gun you used?' Dr. Morelle said. 'Your acquaintance with firearms is no doubt slight, but can you say whether it was an automatic pistol, flat in shape, with the cartridges in a clip in the butt? Or a revolver, with the cartridges in a revolving breech?'

'It was a revolver,' she said. She told him how she had spent the night and the following day; how she had thought of seeking Phil Stone's help, then how she had gone to Aces La Rue. Miss Frayle noticed that Dr. Morelle made no mention of the fact that he had himself made the acquaintance of Phil Stone, at the night-club. It was typical of him, she thought, not to give anything away to anybody more than was absolutely necessary for his own elucidation of the matter that was engaging his attention.

Miss Frayle found herself recalling the silence as the body of the night-club owner was borne out of that sumptuous office, through the almost deserted buildings over which he had held sway, to be whisked through the shadowy streets to a refrigerated compartment in the mortuary, there to await a post-mortem on a cold slab. It was a drab last journey for Ray Mercury who had bossed his little world in Soho with undisputed power.

Inspector Hood and the police experts had still been working over the office, and Miss Frayle had watched Dr. Morelle move to Phil Stone, who stood staring morosely at the spot where Ray Mercury had sprawled.

'You have experienced a somewhat distressing time, Mr. Stone,' he said quietly, 'so recently to have returned to England and to have encountered such dreadful happenings.'

A shadow had passed over the young man's good-looking, sun-burnt face. 'I'd hoped for a — happier leave,' his voice charged with bitterness.

'It was indeed a sad irony of Fate,' Dr. Morelle had said, 'that you should have been the first to discover the poor girl and now this man.'

There had been nothing implied in his tone, though Miss Frayle watching Phil Stone had seen his jaw tighten, and then make a move as if about to say something. Then he had numbly shook his head. It was fortunate for him, Miss Frayle had thought, that Dr. Morelle had estimated that Ray Mercury had been dead at least half an hour before Phil Stone had said he had found him in the office. The police-surgeon who had arrived with the photographer and finger-print experts had put the time of death at the same; and there had been the commissionaire and the waiter to establish that Phil Stone had arrived on the scene, as he said he had, some time after the night-club owner had obviously been dead.

Later Miss Frayle had walked back from Soho, across Oxford Street, to Harley Street, with Dr. Morelle. 'There is nothing more refreshing to the mind than a walk through London's streets in the early hours, Miss Frayle,' he had said. They had left Phil Stone to make his way to his rooms off Baker Street, and to hold himself in readiness to attend the inquest. Inspector Hood had said good night to Dr. Morelle and Miss Frayle at the club-entrance, and looking back she had seen the neon sign still flickering out the words: The Black Moth.

'In any case,' Dr. Morelle was saying to Thelma Grayson, 'it hardly seems to be the sort of thing you would have about the house. How did it come into your possession?'

'I — I borrowed it,' she said.

'From whom?' He noticed her hesitation. 'This is most important,' he said. 'Unless I have your fullest confidence I can't help you.'

'I borrowed it from a man,' she said. 'He often came to the club. He has always been nice to me, I had been out with him two or three times. He's what I suppose you'd call a man-about-town, but I knew he was interested in guns.'

'So you just went and asked him to lend you one, and he did so without question?' Dr. Morelle said drily.

'I told him that there had been one or two attempted burglaries at the cottage, and I was scared, being on my own there, without Julie.'

'What is this man's name and address?' And from the corner of his eye Dr. Morelle saw Miss Frayle's pencil poised over her notebook.

'Tracy Wright,' again that hesitation before she answered him. 'He has a flat in Parkview Court, just off Park Lane.'

Dr. Morelle got up and began slowly to pace up and down. Thelma Grayson watched his tall, gaunt form anxiously. His chin was sunk on his chest, his hands pushed deep into his pockets. She turned to Miss Frayle, who threw her a reassuring little smile. The study was silent, there was no sound of traffic, it might have been a million miles away from anywhere. Thelma's eyes flickered over the crowded book-shelves and the filing-cabinets, and wondered what strange secrets they contained, what other extraordinary confessions had these four walls heard? What other callers on Dr. Morelle had sat here and laid bare their souls to this amazing man?

'You have told me what happened,' Dr. Morelle said to her at last, 'but I should like to know why, having read the suicide report in the newspaper, you didn't decide to stay silent? It would be regarded as suicide, the man you had killed would go tidily to his grave, with your own part in his death unknown.'

'I was appalled by what I'd done,' she said. 'At first, my idea had been to give myself up, to pay the penalty for the crime I'd committed. Then, when I read that it appeared to the police that he had committed suicide, then it seemed I couldn't have shot him.' She broke off, and then continued. 'If I had and they had made a mistake, was it my job to tell them they were wrong? He deserved what he got, would the fact that I confessed to killing him help anybody?'

She hung her head for a few moments. She lifted up her face again and Dr. Morelle studied her, his eyes on hers. He contemplated the tip of his cigarette, watching the smoke spiral upwards. Miss Frayle regarded him over her spectacles, wondering what his decision would be.

'The police have formed their own conclusions,' he said musingly, 'and perhaps no useful purpose would be served by upsetting their theory, at any rate at this moment. I shall be attending the inquest to-morrow, as a matter of fact. Afterwards I will decide whether there is any further information I can usefully contribute to the matter. Meanwhile you may rest assured that you need have no grounds for further anxiety or apprehension for the future. Leave everything to me.'

She stood up and made a move as if to thank him, but his face had suddenly become stern and forbidding. 'Please understand, however, that I do not condone the fact that you took the law into your own hands. Your action was reckless and quite dreadful.'

Thelma Grayson broke down then. Her hands went to her face, and she rocked in her agony of mind. Miss Frayle's notebook fell to the floor as she jumped to her feet, and crossed to the other to pat her shoulder comfortingly.

Dr. Morelle was leaning thoughtfully against the desk, unperturbed by this display of feminine emotion. And then he seemed to tower over Thelma Grayson as he stared hypnotically into her tear-filled eyes.

'There may arise reasons why the circumstances surrounding Ray Mercury's death should be probed a trifle deeper,' he said. 'Even if only on account of your peace of mind.' He smiled at her bleakly, paused, and then added: 'I will prescribe two things for you which should prove beneficial, first a sedative, to be followed by a good night's sleep.'

And he turned to his desk for a piece of notepaper and began to scribble quickly, his face calm and enigmatic beneath the light from the desk lamp.

Chapter Fifteen

Miss Frayle sat at her desk, all the notes Dr. Morelle had dictated to her on the Ray Mercury case staring up at her in a thick heap.

It was the morning following Thelma Grayson's visit, and Dr. Morelle had gone to give his evidence at the inquest upon the late owner of the Black Moth. Miss Frayle had been reading through the typewritten pages, wandering, it seemed to her, deeper into a maze of conflicting notions. How could the Phil Stone story and Thelma Grayson's story fit in?

It was about midday as Miss Frayle puzzled her way through the typewritten pages, that an idea came to her, like a blinding light. Heavens, she thought, her eyes shining, her fingers trembling as she clutched the page she held. She was sure that was it. If that girl told the truth, that explained everything. She must tell Dr. Morelle. She was sure he would see it like this, it was one of her flashes of insight.

Full of excitement at her discovery she jumped up and paced about the study with nervous steps. Presently she heard Dr. Morelle's key in the front door lock, and she hurried out into the hall to greet him. She had not expected him back so soon.

'You're back quickly,' she said. 'What did they decide? Was it —?'

'On the evidence put before them,' Dr. Morelle said, 'the Coroner's jury returned the verdict that Ray Mercury had committed suicide.' As Miss Frayle trotted after him to the study, he went on: 'You must remember that the Coroner was not in the possession of certain facts which as it happens are known to us.'

'Doctor,' she said breathlessly, 'I understand that. Now, there's something —'

Dr. Morelle had entered his study and sat down behind his desk. 'It has been a wearying morning, Miss Frayle,' he said, interrupting her. 'Some coffee, don't you think, before we set to work.'

Miss Frayle burst out. 'I've got an idea. It came to me in a flash, and I'm sure it will solve everything.'

'You astound me,' Dr. Morelle said imperturbably. 'No doubt one of your more highly-coloured flights of imagination. Very interesting, of course, but once again I must remind you that it is only by a process of skilled ratiocination that the truth can be arrived at.'

'But I'm sure Miss Grayson —'

'Coffee, Miss Frayle,' Dr. Morelle said.

Miss Frayle compressed her lips and turned on her heel and marched from the room, the carriage of her head on her slim shoulders showing her sense of frustration. Dr. Morelle smiled after her, and sat thoughtfully. He did not stir from his chair, but remained as if carved from some sort of pulsating metal, until Miss Frayle presently returned with a tray of coffee, hot and with its appetizing aroma. Somewhat mutinously Miss Frayle sat down. Then she relaxed a little as she decided she would bide her time to explode her bombshell and shatter Dr. Morelle's complacent conceit.

'First, we have the undoubted fact, reaffirmed by the evidence at the inquest,' Dr. Morelle said, 'that Ray Mercury was found lying on his back, an automatic pistol near his hand. It was further established that he was shot dead by a bullet from this same pistol. It seemed clear enough, taking into account the suicide-note which the deceased left behind that he had taken his own life.'

'Yes,' Miss Frayle said, 'that all seems clear enough.'

'I am glad that you agree with me,' he said ironically. 'But against all that apparently indisputable evidence, we have Miss Grayson's extraordinary revelations last night, that she had entered the office, and shot him dead. According to her account, the time when she perpetrated this crime fits in with the approximate time of Mercury's death.'

Miss Frayle could sit still no longer. 'That's what I've been trying to tell you,' she said. 'Don't you see,' her glasses slipping down her nose, her hands fluttering agitatedly as she tried to gain his attention, 'it's quite easy to realize what happened.' She broke off for a moment as she caught his sardonic expression bent upon her over his coffee-cup. Then she hurried on. 'She did fire at him, as she said, but — she missed.'

Somehow what she was saying didn't sound as if it was of such epoch-making proportions, after all; her idea was not perhaps such a world-shattering one. He continued to regard her calmly at any rate from under lowered brows. She was acutely disappointed to find that she had not caused the sensation she had expected. In fact, a certain amount of alarm filled her at Dr. Morelle's calm, and a sick feeling took possession of her. She had blundered again.

'I had considered that possibility myself,' Dr. Morelle said coldly, 'and I rejected it.'

Miss Frayle sat back, deflated. She looked at him miserably. 'But it seems so plain, I was quite certain that she hadn't killed him.'

'Miss Frayle,' he said, 'satisfying though your solution might be, I would remind you that the revolver she said she had used, and she was specific in her description of it, would fire a bullet very different from that of the type which killed Ray Mercury. It would have been a heavier-calibre bullet, and there would have been visible damage to the panelling behind the desk where Mercury was standing. Or if her aim had been so that the bullet struck the desk there must have been evidence of it. I myself, in my swift scrutiny of the room, perceived no signs of such evidence. The police, in their more meticulous search, did not find any damage, either, which might have been caused by the bullet, or any sign of the bullet itself. Therefore, Miss Frayle, if Miss Grayson fired, she did not miss.'

'Oh, dear,' Miss Frayle said. 'It does seem clear now that it couldn't have been what I thought it was,' she shook her head dejectedly. 'I can't understand it. It's all so puzzling.'

'A solution might be,' Dr. Morelle said, 'that Miss Grayson lied to us about the type of revolver which she tells us she used, and later so conveniently discarded. That in fact she shot him with the automatic. On the other hand,' he went on, 'it would require that she had learned the nature of the gun which actually had been used, in order to present us with the idea that she had used a totally different type, a revolver. She did not seem to me to be possessed of such a cold-blooded calculating temperament. On the contrary, I am quite certain that she acted as she did in a mood of burning desperation, her judgment clouded, her sole thought being to revenge her sister's death. We may also discard any idea of collusion between her and Stone.'

'You mean they might have worked this together?' Miss Frayle said. The idea had never occurred to her. 'They probably are close,' she said, 'because of her sister.'

Dr. Morelle nodded. 'Quite,' he said, 'and the possibility that the two of them had planned to murder the man and had carried it out together had presented itself. But I rejected it,' he went on, 'for the reason that if that were the case, why did she come to me and re-open the murder when the impression that it was a case of suicide was already attained? No,' he said thoughtfully, 'that is out of the question. We must seek elsewhere, Miss Frayle, if we want to discover the truth.'

'But how can we find out what really happened? Everyone, except us, seems quite happy to leave it as it is. There's no proof to the contrary.'

'There is proof, somewhere,' Dr. Morelle said. 'First I shall look into the question of this revolver that Miss Grayson used.'

Miss Frayle was looking thoughtful again. 'Then there's the suicide-note.'

Dr. Morelle stared at her abstractedly. 'The strange thing is, Miss Frayle,' he said, 'that those who knew Mercury by reputation, such as Inspector Hood, found it hard to believe that he would commit suicide for the reason he gave. I must say that my own views concur with theirs.'

'Then someone else wrote it?'

'That would be the logical inference to be deduced,' Dr. Morelle said. 'It would not prove an impossible task for someone to forge his handwriting.'

Miss Frayle stared at him, her mouth open, her eyes wide. 'Who?' she said.

His gaze was suddenly hooded. 'When we know more about what took place in that office,' he said, 'who was there with Ray Mercury when he met his death, then we shall doubtless discover who wrote the farewell-message. All in good time.'

It took some moments for the full significance of what he had said to sink into Miss Frayle's mind. Then she gasped, and her eyes were bright with excitement, and her hand was again adjusting her slipping horn-rims.

'If somebody wrote it for him,' she said, then broke off. 'Oh, goodness, that means they wanted to make it look like suicide. That somebody, whoever it was, shot him and wrote the note and left the gun in his hand all to give the impression he had shot himself.'

'That is a theory which suggests itself to me,' Dr. Morelle said.

Miss Frayle's mind was dazzled with this new idea. A sobering thought came to her and her face clouded. 'But that means Thelma Grayson might still have done it.'

'Which brings me back to the plan I have in mind,' Dr. Morelle said, rising from his desk. He glanced at his wrist-watch. It was just approaching twelve-thirty. 'You'd better come with me.'

Excitedly, Miss Frayle began tidying her desk, putting the batch of notes she had been poring over in order. She looked out of the window. The September sky was a clear, greyish blue. 'Where are we going?'

'Parkview Court.'

'Parkview Court?' She stared at him, wide-eyed. 'That's where that man Tracy Wright lives. The man who lent her the gun,' she said.

Miss Frayle studied his saturnine features. Was this mysterious Tracy Wright also involved in the death of the owner of the Black Moth? Was Dr. Morelle on to something, was it more than just a theory he had? Did he know something which led him to believe that this was not a case of suicide after all? After all that had gone before, she found this hard to believe, but none knew better than she his uncanny insight into such bewildering puzzles as this was turning out to be.

She longed to discuss the case further with him during the short journey to Parkview Court, but Dr. Morelle had relapsed into one of his enigmatic silences. Her eager questions brought no response from the brooding figure beside her, and she was feeling somewhat frustrated again when the taxi turned into a narrow street off Park Lane and drew up outside an imposing block of flats which towered many storeys up towards the sky.

Chapter Sixteen

Dr. Morelle and Miss Frayle went into a luxuriously carpeted, discreetly-lit foyer and after inquiring from a uniformed porter in an office in the corner, a beautifully panelled lift shot them smoothly to the top floor, and they stepped out into the softly-lit passage. A few yards along a door before them bore a neat brass plate with the name Tracy Wright on it.

Miss Frayle had given up trying to obtain any answers from Dr. Morelle. Excitement surged through her. She felt they were getting somewhere near the solution of the mystery, and she awaited the meeting with Tracy Wright full of expectation.

A thin, urbane-featured manservant answered Dr. Morelle's ring. Dr. Morelle gave his name and asked to see Mr. Wright for a few minutes, and the man went away and returned in a moment or two. 'Mr. Wright will see you, sir,' he said.

Miss Frayle followed Dr. Morelle's tall figure across a hall, showing every sign of sumptuousness and luxury living. It was a penthouse flat. Wide windows in the beautifully furnished room they had entered gave on to a roof garden, and beyond Miss Frayle caught a breathtaking view over rooftops and across Hyde Park.

'Dr. Morelle? I'm Tracy Wright.'

The man at an occasional table turned and putting down a glossy magazine shook hands with Dr. Morelle, and as he did so a light dawned in his eyes. 'Why, of course,' he said with a little smile. 'How stupid of me. I knew your name, but —' He broke off. 'You are the great criminologist, I've heard about you and read a lot about you.'

While Dr. Morelle gave a deprecatory murmur, Miss Frayle was gazing at Tracy Wright. He was tall and slim and dressed in a dark suit. There were lines of dissipation round his eyes, but his face was hard and bronzed. Placing him at somewhere round forty years of age, she guessed that he was a man who lived hard and played hard and who took pride in keeping himself in perfect physical condition. Her gaze, wandering round the room, took in the many sporting prints and hunting trophies. It seemed to her that the round of gaiety which, according to Thelma Grayson, he led in the night-haunts of London must form only part of his existence.

She started as she became aware that he was glancing at her quizzically.

'This is Miss Frayle, my secretary,' said Dr. Morelle.

'Delighted to meet you Miss Frayle.'

Miss Frayle was blushing. 'I do so admire your flat, Mr. Wright,' she said. 'It's absolutely charming.'

'It's a nice spot to come back to,' he said casually. 'I travel a lot, you know.' He smiled at them as the manservant came softly into the room. He waited until the drinks had been brought and then with a smile full of charm he said to Dr. Morelle: 'Since your secretary's here, I take it this is a business call. I can't imagine what the business is.'

He had become suddenly wary, Miss Frayle thought, and she sat quivering, sipping her beautifully-cut glass of sherry to hide her excitement.

'I am engaged in an investigation,' said Dr. Morelle suavely, 'and it occurred to me that you can help me. And so on an impulse I thought I would call in the hope that you would see me.'

Wright's eyebrows rose, and he stared at Dr. Morelle. 'I've been behaving myself lately,' he said, that charming smile in evidence once more, 'and I haven't run across any bad lads of the town.'

'That wasn't in my mind, Mr. Wright,' Dr. Morelle's voice remained light as he appeared to change the subject. 'What a charming photograph you have over there.'

Tracy Wright turned, his jaw suddenly taut. 'Thelma Grayson? Yes, a nice girl.'

He said it casually enough, but Miss Frayle, who had not spotted the photograph until Dr. Morelle drew her attention to it, noticed that Tracy Wright had tensed, and again she experienced that quivering thrill of excitement. She observed that there were a number of photographs of other pretty young women scattered about. He was obviously quite a man for the girls, she thought.

'You know Miss Grayson well?' Dr. Morelle was saying, conversationally.

The other shrugged. 'We've met on and off, he said, 'and got on well together.' He glanced shrewdly at Dr. Morelle. 'You know her, too? And you've come to see me about something which concerns her?' Wright said.

He paused and glanced out of the window and then back to Dr. Morelle. 'Not about that dreadful affair of her sister?'

'You are making my task easier,' Dr. Morelle said, watching him.

'Really?' Wright said, and looked startled, and again Miss Frayle saw the wariness in his expression. 'What are you driving at?'

'You remarked that you know Miss Grayson fairly well.' Dr. Morelle had thrown a glance at the photograph in the leather frame. He glanced at Tracy Wright again. 'Well enough to lend her a revolver?'

The other stared at him. 'So that's it,' he said. 'The gun.' Abruptly his tone changed. He frowned. 'You're not telling me she's made a fool of herself with that?'

'You have some knowledge of guns?'

Tracy Wright smiled. 'My hobby, you might say. I've got quite a collection. Perhaps you'd like to look at it?'

Dr. Morelle and Miss Frayle followed him, Miss Frayle spilling a little of her drink as she set her glass on a low table. They went through a wide doorway into a smaller room, and Miss Frayle looked around her with interest. Round the light-oak panelled walls firearms of all kinds were displayed. There were old-fashioned rifles and modern shotguns, big-game rifles, and plenty of examples of the art of early gunsmiths.

Tracy Wright turned from a 12-gauge wildfowl gun and picked up a flintlock holster pistol which lay with a collection of other flintlocks on a table. 'This pistol is in fine condition,' he said, holding it for Dr. Morelle to see. 'The barrel and lock have a browned finish caused by a thin film of rust which has become highly-polished by constant rubbing of the part of its former owners. Whether or not this browning is the original finish of the pistol it's impossible to say, although browning is, of course, oxidation produced by water or acid and highly polished.' Dr. Morelle nodded understandingly, while the other went on. 'I'm inclined to think the browning is original, the engraving at the baluster turn is deep and clear.'

He indicated a strawberry motif delicately engraved on the barrel. Miss Frayle found herself completely unable to follow as Tracy Wright continued with rising enthusiasm: 'The frizzen pan,' he said, 'is of the detachable type and has been renewed at an early date in the gun's career. I'd describe it as a semi-military pistol, because of the fine workmanship. You can see how the barrel tang is secured by a screw, the head of which is under the trigger-guard, a neat arrangement, met with on early pieces, but soon to disappear because of the nuisance in dismantling for cleaning purposes. The barrel is pinned to the stock with round steel pins; the side nails securing the lock are massive, round, square-headed screws, undoubtedly genuine. There is no bridle to the tumbler inside the lock or to the frizzen pan. The lack of a bridle to the tumbler is a curious feature on so fine a weapon, and makes me think it's much earlier than 1702, but at the same time it cannot be as old as 1645, which is the date the bridle was supposed to have been used for the first time in this country.'

Dr. Morelle murmured understandingly, once more though Miss Frayle thought she detected a slightly glazed look in his eyes, even he was surely finding this spate of information on such an obscure subject a bit overwhelming?

'The wood of the stock, being English field maple,' Tracy Wright was saying, 'is unusual. As you can see, the wood is short-grained and brittle, not really suitable for firearms. The old fallacy that these pistols had a large ball butt so that they could be used as a club in a close fight is nonsense; one blow with it would smash it to pieces, and at the price of firearms in those days no one could afford such a luxury.'

Tracy Wright smiled a sudden charming smile at Miss Frayle. 'But I'm sure all this talk about guns must be boring you?'

'Not at all,' she said politely. 'I don't mind a bit as long as they don't go off.'

'Mr. Wright,' Dr. Morelle said quietly, 'don't you think it was risky to lend Miss Grayson a loaded revolver?'

Tracy Wright put down the flintlock and turned to him coolly. 'You're being pretty cagey with me,' he said. 'I agree with you she asked me to lend her a gun. So I lent her one. A Smith and Wesson Centennial, a hammerless-job, it fires a .38 calibre cartridge.' For a moment Miss Frayle thought he was going to launch into another description of the gun, but he paused and merely said. 'That's all, quite simple. If that's what you've come to ask, there it is.'

Miss Frayle watched him as he went to a big carved chest-of-drawers. He came back with a small polished wooden box which rattled as he shook it, and opened the lid. From it he took a handful of gleaming cartridges and showed them to Dr. Morelle in his palm before letting them drop back into the box.

'These are the sort of cartridges I gave her with it.'

'I see,' said Dr. Morelle thoughtfully, his gaze still on the contents of the box. 'Most illuminating.'

'I only let her have three rounds,' went on Tracy Wright. 'Actually I thought she was being a bit alarmist about this burglar scare at her cottage, but she kept on about it, and although she admitted she didn't know a great deal about handling a revolver, I imagined it would give her confidence.'

'That was very thoughtful of you,' Dr. Morelle said.

'She's been through a tough time lately, and I wanted to cheer her up a bit.'

A little while later, after what to Miss Frayle seemed to have been a most fruitless visit, she and Dr. Morelle were descending in the quietly humming lift, and were on the pavement outside Parkview Court looking for a taxi.

'I don't understand,' Miss Frayle was saying to Dr. Morelle. 'That man didn't tell us anything. He was quite nice, I thought. Very handsome and charming. Even if he did go on a bit about his guns, I really thought he was like a gramophone that would never run down. But we don't know any more now about what we wanted to know than we did before.'

Dr. Morelle glanced at her with a faint gleam of amusement in his expression. A taxi drew up and they got in, still without his answering her question. He leaned back in the taxi and lit a Le Sphinx. She saw the tantalizing look on his face and gave a sigh of exasperation.

Whatever it was Dr. Morelle had learned from their visit to Tracy Wright, he was not going to impart it to her, yet.

Chapter Seventeen

As Ray Mercury's lawyer, Larry Bellairs had met Greta Mercury only occasionally. He had been impressed by her good looks, but somewhat chilled by the off-hand manner in which she accepted his compliments. Now, this afternoon, following the inquest on Bellairs' client, when Mercury's widow called at his office he was delighted to see her.

With admiration he watched her lithe movements as she came into his large, tastefully appointed office, with its valuable oil-paintings on the walls, and the muted roar of the traffic from Shaftesbury Avenue surging through a partly-opened window.

A plump man in impeccable black jacket and striped trousers, he extended a pudgy hand to her. His manner was a suitable mingling of deference and friendliness. His unblinking eyes were cold and light coloured against his ivory complexion and smoothly brushed back hair.

'It must have been an ordeal, the inquest,' he said with a sorrowful shake of his head. He indicated an early edition of the evening paper on his desk, which carried the story on the front page, with the jury's verdict.

'I didn't have to answer many questions,' Greta Mercury said coolly. 'I just had to give evidence of identity.'

'Yes, yes,' Bellairs shivered slightly, surprised if not faintly shocked at her chill manner. 'I suppose they wanted to know whether he was happy, and so on?'

'I told them all I could,' she said with a slight smile. 'They asked me when I'd last seen him, and I told them that it had been in the club, some time before he was found dead. Of course, they wanted to know whether I knew of any reason why he should have taken his life.' She shrugged. 'Well, I just couldn't say much. After all they had the note, and that was plain enough. I suppose they had to show sympathy, but they must have known I wasn't exactly pleased that he'd shot himself over some girl.'

He saw a glitter in her eyes. He gave a little cough, and wondered what her visit was in aid of.

Greta Mercury was thinking that despite his air of respectability and the opulence of his office Larry Bellairs was as sharp and shady a lawyer as could be found. Her husband often had, she knew, good reason to thank him for his nimble wits, and his intricate knowledge of the loopholes in the law, his alertness and devotion to the interests of his clients. He'd done well out of Ray Mercury, Ray had often said it was worth paying that shark lawyer, as he termed him privately, for the services he rendered.

'Frankly,' she was saying, 'I don't like people pointing at me and saying there's Mrs. Mercury whose husband ran around after any doll that took his fancy, and killed himself because of one of them.'

Bellairs coughed delicately. He was getting an insight into the nature of this woman which had not been revealed to him before. There was venom in her deep, throaty voice, and it startled him a little, while exciting him at the thought of the smouldering fires that burned beneath her icy exterior. He would like to get to know her better, he told himself.

'I came to see you to find out how I stand,' she said.

'Yes,' he nodded slowly, thinking she hadn't wasted much time. 'Naturally.'

'I thought of getting away for a while,' she said. 'Soon as I could. The South of France. It's been a shock, all this. But I'd like to know how I stand before I go.' She paused and looked at him steadily. 'He never told me everything, but he had a profitable racket and there ought to be something left for me.'

'Ray has left you comfortably off,' he assured her.

'That's good to hear,' she said, and there was a curiously cynical tone in her voice. 'How much did he leave me?'

'Twenty thousand,' he said, 'and nicely salted away. If you leave all the — ah — arrangements to me, you'll get it all clear of tax or anything like that.' He gave another little cough. 'And then there's the Black Moth.'

'The Black Moth,' she said non-committally. 'What about it?'

'I don't know what your plans for that may be,' the lawyer said. 'You may want to continue to run it, or sell out. It's all yours to decide. Again, I suggest you leave all that to me, when you've made up your mind.'

'It's funny,' she said, 'to think of that place belonging to me. I always hated it. It came between me and him.' And suddenly she launched into a soft-voiced, unemotional, but bitter tirade of abuse against the club and its late owner's associates, while Larry Bellairs gaped at her in astonishment. What a woman. What fire. Like a tigress, he thought. He'd thought how it would be delightful to know her better, but on second thoughts, he decided it would also be dangerous.

'I can dispose of it all right,' he said. 'If that is what you want.' He was bending over her, and his moist hand rested on hers. 'Remember I'm your friend,' he said insinuatingly. 'If there is any way in which I can help you, please let me know.'

Her white hot fury subsided, though her eyes still glittered as she looked up at him mockingly. 'I was thinking,' she said, 'that not only might you be a bit of a shark, but a bit of a wolf also. I never suspected it of you.'

The other smiled unabashed. 'You are an extremely attractive young woman,' he said warmly. 'And I will be glad to help you.'

'We'll talk about that some time,' she said, in her deep, throaty tones. 'We'll decide what to do about the club, when I come back.' Her eyes hardened again, and he felt her hand move spasmodically under his.

'I shall always be around,' he said softly.

The telephone on his desk buzzed discreetly and he picked up the receiver, to listen to the voice of his clerk.

'Inspector Hood?' he said. Again he listened. 'Tell him to wait a moment. I'll see him.'

He hung up, irritated by the interruption of his intriguing conversation with Greta Mercury, and a little apprehensive about the inspector's call. He knew Inspector Hood through various police-court cases, what was he doing here? Thoughtfully he glanced at Greta Mercury. She was leaning forward tensely.

'Police?' she said, in a whisper. 'What are they after?'

'I can't say,' he said.

'Is it about Ray?'

'How could it be about Ray? The Coroner's court returned their verdict. That's all finished.'

She stared at a spot over his shoulder, her gaze unseeing. Then she stood up and held out her hand, which he held for a long time. He ushered her to the door and watched her hips as she went through to the outer office. Inspector Hood, sitting comfortably in a chair, his big hands on his knees, his unlit pipe drooping from his mouth, also watched her go, not without interest.

He came into Bellairs' office with a somewhat chilly greeting to the lawyer, and took the chair he offered. He didn't like Larry Bellairs, and the other knew it.

'Ray Mercury's widow wasn't it?' Hood said.

'You saw her at the inquest, you are well aware who she is. Poor girl. It's been a great shock to her.'

'If I was her I shouldn't be sorry to see him go.'

'That is hardly the thing to say of a recently bereaved widow,' Bellairs said.

'Depends on the husband — and the wife,' Inspector Hood said. 'Smoke my pipe, if you don't mind,' as the other offered him a cigar from a box he produced out of his desk-drawer. Bellairs' nostrils quivered as the acrid smoke drifted across to him. Still busy with his match Hood growled: 'I'm just looking into one or two things about Ray Mercury. Routine stuff, that's all.'

The other looked warily at the burly police officer, whose bubbling pipe sent more smoke-clouds wreathing between them. 'As his lawyer,' he said, 'you'll realize my business with him was confidential. But if there is any matter in which I can help you I, as his lawyer, will be glad to.'

The detective eyed him sceptically, and Bellairs wondered what he had been driving at. None knew better than he that there were plenty of disreputable facets to his late client's career. What line was Inspector Hood following? Would it affect him? Or Greta? His thoughts lingered on the pale hair, her supple figure and her throaty voice.

'Let's get it straight,' Inspector Hood said. 'We know he was linked with one or two things which we don't like. The fact that he's out of our reach now, doesn't mean that we're not still interested in these things.'

'What do you want to know, and why do you think I should be able to help you?' Bellairs brought his thoughts back from his vision of Greta Mercury and settled them on the less attractive figure before him.

'I was just wondering what was going to happen to the Black Moth,' the detective-inspector said. 'Who gets it now? You, for instance?'

The lawyer smiled. 'Why should I have it?' he said. 'I had nothing to do with running the place, I had no interest in it. I was Ray Mercury's lawyer, that was all. Not his business-partner.'

Inspector Hood looked at him, his pipe-bowl gurgling noisily. 'So you were just his lawyer,' he said. 'You never mixed up in any of his enterprises.' He considered this for a moment. 'So the club belongs to who, now?'

'His widow.'

'And is she going to carry on the place?'

The other shrugged. 'She came in to see me about it,' he said. 'That and other matters relating to her husband's will. But we didn't discuss the future of the Black Moth. It'll wait till she comes back.'

'Back from where? Where's she going?'

'Abroad, I believe,' the lawyer said. 'But I don't think her plans are fixed at the moment.'

Inspector Hood nodded. He rose to his feet with a little grunt. Bellairs watched him, his expression masked by a fixed smile, a smile with little humour in it. 'So she may decide to keep the place going, or sell out?'

The lawyer nodded. 'She'll make up her mind when she returns. I can't tell you what she'll do.'

'And you'll be looking after her interests?' the detective said. He moved slowly to the door. 'You see,' he said, 'I always wanted to put Ray Mercury where he belonged while he was alive. He's dead now, committed suicide,' he paused to take his pipe out of his mouth and regard the blackened bowl with careful interest, 'so I can't very well do much about him. But it was from the Black Moth that he operated his less respectable activities, and I was just wondering if Greta Mercury took over the place if she'd take over her late husband's dope-running business as well.'

Inspector Hood shot the lawyer a look from under his heavy brows. The other stood at his desk and said nothing. He watched the detective go out, leaving behind him an acrid plume of tobacco-smoke gouting from his pipe, and a vague feeling of apprehension in Larry Bellairs' mind.

Chapter Eighteen

Inspector Hood turned up at 221B Harley Street that afternoon.

Miss Frayle still frustrated by Dr. Morelle's intriguing silence since their return from their visit to Tracy Wright, answered the door. Inspector Hood explained that he had decided to have a chat with Dr. Morelle after leaving Larry Bellairs, before going on to Scotland Yard. Inspector Hood was always pleased to call at the house in Harley Street. He remembered with warmth the quiet of the study, conducive to calm thought and reasoned recapitulation. There with the help of Dr. Morelle's acute brain, he had resolved many a problem that had nagged him in the past.

In his present task no great matter of deduction was involved, it called for painstaking police-work, plodding from place to place, from link to link. But, all the same, he welcomed the idea of talking things over with Dr. Morelle.

'Why so interested, Inspector?' Dr. Morelle was asking him now. 'After all this creature Mercury is dead.'

Hood was busy with his inevitable pipe. His keen eyes, under their heavy brows, regarded Dr. Morelle through a haze of smoke, while Miss Frayle had settled herself behind her desk. She listened with interest to the man from Scotland Yard and Dr. Morelle discussing the Black Moth business. She hoped Dr. Morelle might reveal to the detective what he had so far abstained from disclosing to her, especially the result of their visit to Tracy Wright.

'I'll go back a bit,' said Inspector Hood presently. 'Some time ago a girl of a very good family ended up in a nursing home as a hopeless drug-addict. Nothing special about that, maybe. But she was one of a series of similar cases. She had been a familiar figure round the night-clubs, especially the Black Moth. Like the other women, some young and some old enough to know better. The whole business was handled quietly from the publicity point of view, for the sake of the girl and her family. But it began to make us think even more closely about Ray Mercury. We'd been after the pipeline along which the distribution of drugs went on, for a long time, and everything was pointing to the Black Moth.'

'A familiar and unhappy situation,' Dr. Morelle said. 'Yet you found nothing definite to go on, so far as this man Mercury was concerned?'

Inspector Hood shook his head. 'Not so far. He covered his tracks well. He worked through associates, naturally, and I haven't been able to pin them down yet. Now Mercury is no longer with us, but what we want to know is who's taking over from him. He must have built up a profitable business, dope isn't bought for pennies, and somebody must have been all set to muscle in.'

Miss Frayle shuddered as grim and macabre visions of dope-traffickeers and their victims, all she'd heard about them, came to her mind.

'He had a wife,' Dr. Morelle was saying. 'I saw her at the inquest, didn't I? A beautiful and self-possessed young woman.'

'Tough and as hard as nails,' said Hood. 'She's got the club,' he went on. 'Mercury's lawyer, a shady type called Larry Bellairs, told me. She was just leaving when I arrived there. He couldn't, or wouldn't, tell me if she's going to run the joint herself.' He paused and puffed at his pipe. 'And also what I'm wondering,' he said, 'is if she'll keep a man named Luke Roper, who went with the club, as you might say. Mercury's right-hand hatchet-man, he was. Whether she knew about, or is interested in, her late husband's dope-racket, is another matter.'

'This man Roper, he was close to Mercury?' Dr. Morelle said.

Hood shrugged. 'They were as friendly as two men can be who are watching each other all the time like cobras.'

'Is he a criminal?'

Inspector Hood nodded. 'He's done one or two stretches, but he's as slippery as a snake. A dangerous baby, if ever there was one. One of these quiet, self-contained characters who never blabs around about what he's doing. Always got a grip on himself.'

Dr. Morelle lit a Le Sphinx, and its fragrant aroma mingled with the nostril-stinging fumes of Hood's pipe. 'Your surmise is that Roper may be planning to carry on with the narcotics business either on his own, or with Mercury's widow?'

'That is feasible,' Hood said. He stood up, stretching slowly. 'Many thanks for the chat, I'll be on my weary way, plodding along like the poor flat-footed copper I am. If you get any bright ideas, I'd be glad to have them.'

Miss Frayle caught the enigmatic look that flickered across Dr. Morelle's face. She glimpsed a momentary gleam in his hooded eyes.

'I'm delighted you called,' Dr. Morelle said.

At the hall-door, as she saw him out, Hood clutched his black trilby and whispered to Miss Frayle: 'What's he up to? He's interested in this Black Moth business, I can sniff it a mile off. And when Dr. Morelle's interested, he isn't doing it for the hell of it.'

Miss Frayle fluttered. 'I really don't know Inspector,' she said. 'His brain works much too fast for me.'

Hood chuckled. 'The old thought-processes that he's so fond of talking about, eh?'

After he had gone Miss Frayle went back to find Dr. Morelle smiling bleakly to himself as his gaze wandered idly round the bookshelves lining the study walls.

'What did you make of that?' she said brightly.

'Inspector Hood vouchsafed me an interesting item or two,' Dr. Morelle said. 'I think it would prove instructive to learn more about Ray Mercury's widow, and about this man Luke Roper.'

'What I meant was, why didn't you mention anything to him about Tracy Wright?' she said. 'And you never dropped a hint about what Thelma Grayson told us. I'm sure he would have been terribly thrilled to hear about all that.'

Dr. Morelle considered her thoughtfully. The waning September sunlight, pale and a reminder of approaching autumn, shafted through the windows, and the remains of Inspector Hood's tobacco-smoke drifted listlessly ceiling-wards. Somewhere along Harley Street a taxi hooted, the faint mutter of traffic from Marylebone Road obtruded intermittently upon the silence of the study.

'What, regrettably, you have not yet learned, Miss Frayle,' Dr. Morelle said at last, 'is that there is a time to speak and a time to remain silent. There is no danger attached to the fact that while Thelma Grayson believes she murdered Ray Mercury, the police believe he died by his own hand. Because I happen to know the truth is of no consequence to anyone, except the woman who thinks she is a murderess, and she will know what I know all in good time.'

'You — you mean you know for certain she didn't kill him?' Miss Frayle had leapt towards Dr. Morelle and now she stood staring up at him, her teeth chattering with excitement.

Dr. Morelle nodded and permitted himself an indulgent smile at Miss Frayle who was clutching at his arm. 'I am positive she did not murder him,' she said.

Now she was frowning and biting her lower lip as she tried to recall what it was she had missed during their visit to the penthouse overlooking Hyde Park. What had Tracy Wright said which had obviously clinched the matter for Dr. Morelle? She voiced her thoughts aloud.

'I can't think what he said which gave you a clue,' she said. 'Any clue at all.'

'He?' His expression struck her as being ostentatiously puzzled, and she was filled with a wave of frustration inspired by his complacency.

'Tracy Wright,' she said. 'I never heard him utter a word which seemed to me to help us, so far as Thelma Grayson was concerned.'

'I recall your mentioning the fact, Miss Frayle,' he said.

'What did he say, then? He rattled on for hours about his blessed old guns; and he admitted what we already knew, what she'd told us, that he'd lent her the gun to shoot Ray Mercury with. But what else?'

Dr. Morelle smiled at her condescendingly. 'You are suffering from the assumption,' he said, 'that it was the interview with Tracy Wright which resulted in my reaching the conclusion that Thelma Grayson had not committed murder.'

Her eyes were round behind her horn-rimmed spectacles. 'But isn't that what you said?' she said. 'Isn't that what you meant?'

Slowly he shook his head. 'I knew that she hadn't fired the fatal shot before we called at Parkview Court,' he said.

'Then why did you —?' she began to say, then broke off, and asked him instead: 'How did you know?' she said.

'Thelma Grayson herself told us.'

'Thelma Grayson —?'

Again she broke off in mid-sentence and stared at him, a baffled expression spreading over her face. She shook her head, and turned away from him, to throw herself into a chair. 'I give up,' she said.

'You were here at the time,' he said. 'You were listening to her.' He moved to his desk and took a fresh Le Sphinx from the skull cigarette-box. Every line of his tall, gaunt frame infuriated her, every nuance in his voice. How could she possibly have missed hearing what Thelma Grayson had said? She had sat there listening with rapt attention.

The flame of his lighter threw the high cheekbones of his brooding features into relief. He drew at his cigarette for a moment and then said through a cloud of smoke: 'You also saw the deceased in his office at the night-club.'

She sat up in her chair. 'What's that got to do with it?' she said. She had a vision of that inert figure lying on the floor as she had burst into Ray Mercury's office that night in search of Dr. Morelle.

'Don't you recall the position of the body?' Dr. Morelle said.

'Of course,' she said. 'I remember quite well. But I don't see —?'

'Cast your mind back.'

'I have,' she said. 'The poor thing was in a heap, lying by his desk. I remember it perfectly well. And you and Inspector Hood were there.'

'And when Thelma Grayson told us so vividly how she had gone into the office and shot him,' he said, 'didn't anything strike you about her description as somewhat significant?'

She scowled to herself, her brow corrugated above her spectacles, as she tried to fathom what he was getting at. She summed up all her powers of concentration as she sought to remember, word by word, Thelma Grayson's account of those dramatic moments. Nothing stirred in her consciousness to convey to her any hint of what Dr. Morelle was talking about.

''He was frightened,' was what she said,' Dr. Morelle was saying, ''and tried to come round the desk to me,' do you remember?' Miss Frayle nodded and he continued: 'She went on,' he said, 'by saying: 'and I fired. He fell across the desk sprawling.''

Miss Frayle could hear Thelma Grayson's voice once again in her mind. Yes, that was what she had said. Then Dr. Morelle was speaking. 'And I asked her,' he said, 'if, after she had shot him as she had described it, and he had fallen across the desk, had she touched him? And what did she say?'

'Say?' Miss Frayle blinked at him, and tried to remember, biting her lower lip in her effort. 'What did she say?'

'What answer did she give?' Dr. Morelle paused, and for a moment she had the impression, one which she had experienced on previous occasions, that he was looming before her like some giant, dark bird of prey, about to pounce.

'I'm just thinking,' Miss Frayle said.

Dr. Morelle's mouth tightened in a thin line, and then he said: ''No,' she said, 'I saw what I had done, and remember putting the gun in my pocket, and I went out.' That was what she said.'

A great flash of revelation illuminated Miss Frayle's mind and she jumped up. 'And yet you'd found his body *lying on the floor.*' she said, gulping in her excitement.

'I am gratified to see that the light has at last dawned,' Dr. Morelle said. 'Precisely. She left him for dead, sprawled across his desk, but Inspector Hood and I found Ray Mercury dead on the floor. That was also how Phil Stone and the waiter had come upon him a few minutes before our arrival on the scene. What was the conclusion to be arrived at from those facts?'

'That the body had moved,' Miss Frayle said promptly.

Dr. Morelle eyed her humourlessly. Then he gave a nod. 'It could not have moved itself,' he said, 'if what Thelma Grayson said was true, and she had no possible motive for lying.'

'So someone else must have moved it,' Miss Frayle said, not without an air of triumph.

'Furthermore, we know,' Dr. Morelle said, 'that the bullet which killed the deceased was from the automatic pistol in his hand, and not the revolver Thelma Grayson used.' He tapped the ash off his cigarette into an ash-tray on his desk.

'But I don't understand,' Miss Frayle said. 'She said she shot him and he fell dead.' She paused, while Dr. Morelle regarded her with a bleakly mocking smile. 'And all this about a different bullet from a different gun that was in Ray Mercury's hand —' She found herself unable to conclude the sentence and let the words drift into a puzzled mutter.

'That was a somewhat mystifying feature,' Dr. Morelle said. 'And that was why I decided that a visit to the individual who had lent her the revolver might prove fruitful.'

'But why, if you already knew she hadn't done it?'

'Merely to make assurance doubly sure,' Dr. Morelle said, 'and because I dislike loose strings lying untidily about.'

'And what Tracy Wright told you tied it all up for you?'

Dr. Morelle nodded and took a deep drag at his Le Sphinx. 'Precisely,' he said.

A baffled look was settling over Miss Frayle's face as she tried to remember anything that Tracy Wright might have said which had so impressed Dr. Morelle, to the extent that he was completely reassured that what Thelma Grayson had told him was one hundred per cent true. She thought in vain, and gave it up as Dr. Morelle went on to say: 'It was not so much what he said, but what I saw.'

'I didn't see anything.' Miss Frayle said, 'only a lot of old guns. Although it was a beautiful flat, of course, with that nice manservant and everything. Oh, and there was that photograph of Thelma Grayson.'

She glanced at Dr. Morelle but he failed to look as she had anticipated. 'You did not look,' he said. 'He admitted that he had lent her the gun, for the reason she gave us. He confirmed that it was a Smith and Wesson Centennial, which fitted in with her description of the firearm.'

'And you never told him she'd lost it,' Miss Frayle said.

'That wasn't what seemed important to me,' Dr. Morelle said.

'He's certainly got plenty more.'

'What did interest me,' Dr. Morelle said, with an air of someone exercising great patience, 'was the box of cartridges he produced, three rounds of which he had given Thelma Grayson in the revolver.'

'I didn't bother to look at them,' Miss Frayle said. 'What was there interesting about them, anyway?'

Dr. Morelle contemplated her for a moment through a cloud of cigarette-smoke. 'Merely this,' he said, 'that they were blanks.'

Chapter Nineteen

The day previously Phil Stone had caught a late afternoon train from Waterloo. As he found a third-class smoker to himself and pushed his battered leather suitcase on the rack he was irresistibly recalling the occasion when he had made his first journey to Little Tiplow.

Was it only a bare nine days ago when he had sat back in the corner of a railway-compartment as he was doing now, and filled his pipe from his worn tobacco-pouch? It seemed a lifetime. A lifetime in which it seemed to him that what had transpired had happened not to him but someone else. He had lived in a nightmare.

There came the shrill whistle of the guard, the slamming of carriage-doors, and the train began to move. Phil shifted in his seat and he could feel his wallet in his inside pocket, the wallet in which he knew was the photograph of the girl he had journeyed so far to see. This time he did not take the photograph out to look at it. This time he did not want to be reminded of the girl he loved, but who was dead.

About an hour-and-a-half it would take him to Hatford, he recollected, and then the wait for the local that would carry him to Little Tiplow.

He picked up the early edition of the evening newspaper he had bought at the station bookstall, and tried to concentrate his thoughts on the headlines and print as the train began to speed through the suburbs which lay beneath the bright sky of September's closing days.

Phil Stone had called at Thelma Grayson's flat that afternoon, after he had phoned her earlier in the day and she had asked him to come and see her. The sheer need to talk to somebody he knew about Julie had driven him along to see Thelma. She had greeted him warmly, but as he sat in the small flat, he watched her curiously. She was jumpy and restless, and it was obvious she was still in a state of nervous tension.

'I'm sorry, Phil,' she said noticing his attention on her. 'I shan't really be settled until all this is finished.'

He had stared at her. 'But it is finished. Nothing could be more finished and done with. Not only Julie, but the man who drove her to her death as well. It's all tied up, it couldn't have ended more satisfactorily all round.'

She heard the bitterness in his voice, saw it in his face and breathed a silent prayer of thankfulness that he had been too concerned with his own grief to seize upon the slip she had made.

'I know, it's been dreadful for you,' she said, swiftly, recovering herself and taking advantage of his reaction to what she had told him.

His eyes were still shadowed as he said: 'Best thing for me is to get back to sea again, that'll help me forget.' He paused and then went on, forcing a lightness into his tone: 'I'm afraid I'm being dreadfully selfish, going on about how I feel. It hasn't been so clever for you, either.'

She nodded absently. She wondered what he would say if he knew just how terrible it had been, if he knew that she herself had nursed murder in her heart. Her thoughts went back to her visit to Harley Street last night, and her heart filled with gratitude towards Dr. Morelle for the way he had given her hope and courage. She longed to know what further news he would have for her.

'The strange thing is,' Thelma heard Phil saying, 'I've got a feeling I ought to go to Little Tiplow again. Something seems to be drawing me there. Perhaps it would be painful — but I can't hold myself back.'

Thelma's eyes clouded. 'I know how you feel,' she said softly. 'I think you should go, if you want to, Phil. After all, if you're leaving England again —'

She left the remark unfinished. No need to tell him that this might be his last farewell to Julie.

There was the same hollow-sounding bridge which he had to cross to another platform when he got out at Hatford, grabbing his suitcase. The same fussy little local arrived in due course to take him to Little Tiplow, two or three coaches, no more, rattling into the station. An empty carriage for him again, and he was leaning back in a corner, lighting his pipe, and then the train chugging out.

Last time, Phil remembered, the train to Little Tiplow had been considerably delayed, while he had paced the platform with a watchful eye at the lowering sky. Now, as he glanced out of the window at the passing fields, the sky was clear, with a hint of the approaching evening.

Once more the train rattled into the halt and Phil got out and stood alone on the tiny platform. The same gangling porter bobbed out of the ticket-office, took his ticket, looked at him with a faint smile of recognition, a look which turned to one of curiosity as Phil passed through the gate and set out for the village.

This time there was no storm, no howling wind and driving rain, as Phil Stone went along the village street, serene under the slanting rays of some pale evening sunshine, and there was no sign of life except a prowling dog, which sniffed at his heels, one or two old people who gave Phil a casual glance, and a group of children who smiled at him.

The affair at Lilac Cottage might have been only a momentary sensation in the long and serene life of Little Tiplow.

The landlord of the Half Moon Inn, where he was going to stay, greeted him with a slow smile.

'Nice to see you again, Mr. Stone.' And only a brief silence during which remembering went on, then a word about the weather and Phil was finding his way up the crooked stairs to his low-ceilinged, comfortable bedroom, which overlooked the triangular village-green. He had occupied this room before.

It was good to be among quiet-living people, Phil thought, as he quickly unpacked his suitcase, after the side of life he had touched in recent days.

Half an hour later Phil went out of the inn. He walked down the village street, turning off near the end of the winding, tree-shadowed lane that led in the direction of the cemetery.

Presently, he came to the beginning of the cart-track with the wire-fencing on either side, and went along it, remembering the last time he had been this way on the afternoon of the funeral. He recalled the ostentatious wreath of red roses which Ray Mercury had sent. He was remembering again how he'd wanted to tear the wreath apart, and had been stopped from doing so by Thelma.

And now Ray Mercury was lying in his own grave.

He went on past the houses on either side of the track, lights were beginning to glimmer in the windows. He came to where the track forked and he took the left-hand fork along which he proceeded for about fifty yards. Then it opened out into a small space, and he went over to the low gate, beyond which he could see the white gravestones.

The cemetery appeared empty as he made his way along the path towards Julie's grave. There was no sound but the cawing of rooks, quarrelling among some high elms which overlooked a long field from which the harvest had been gathered, leaving it bare to the evening sky.

He came to the corner where the grave was, and stood looking down at the simple headstone and thoughts crowded in on him, pictures of the happy times he had spent with Julie when she was alive. Emotion caught at his throat, as he recalled how he had found her not so very long ago, dead.

No longer did he feel the anger that had raged through him at the thought of the man who had caused her death.

With a few murmured words, he turned away, knowing that he might never come back again to Julie's last resting-place. Hard though it would be for him, he must draw a curtain on this part of his life. There lay ahead the sea and ships and forgetfulness.

Like a man in a dream he went out of the gate, noticing from the corner of his eye shadowy figures. But no one approached him, or spoke to him. He went some way up the track and then turned through another gate on to a field-path. He knew this led to Lilac Cottage, for he had come back from the cemetery that way with Thelma on the day of the funeral.

Skirting fields and coppices, his mind busy with his thoughts, he made towards the lonely cottage, standing isolated from the village.

He walked faster now, for the shadows were lengthening and soon he stood outside the gate, facing the empty lifeless cottage, white and low-built, its beams showing black in the faint dusk, the porch shadowed a little, the blank windows on either side, the lilac-tree in the corner of the small, hedged garden.

Phil shivered slightly. He had no wish to go in. The place affected him with its air of brooding, and he would not have trusted his emotions if he had been able to step through the door and into the room where Julie had died.

'What are you doing here?' a voice behind him said.

Phil spun round with a slight start. He had heard no sound of footsteps. His eyes narrowed at the man who stood there. Wiry, with a long, swarthy face and dark side-whiskers which reached well below his ears. The cap on the back of his head showed lank black hair, and he wore gumboots over old flannel trousers. His long check jacket, of heavy material, was wide-skirted, and Phil suspected that it hid large pockets. There was bright intelligence in his dark eyes, with their yellowish whites.

'I might ask you the same thing,' Phil said to him with a grin.

The stranger smiled, showing surprisingly white teeth.

'I often passes here, on me way home,' he said coolly.

'You live around here, then?'

The man jerked a thumb over his shoulder. 'Down there in the woods.' He jerked a thumb again, this time at Lilac Cottage. 'I've often helped them with eggs, or a chicken when they wanted one. What's going to happen to the place? I mean, after that business — the poor girl — will the other sister stay on, or is it up for sale?'

As Phil gave him a non-committal shrug, the other suddenly said: 'Truth to tell, I thought you was that other feller come back.'

'Other fellow?'

'Chap who was here on the night of the storm,' the man said, looking up at Phil, with his bright, curious eyes.

For a moment Phil thought the man must be making a mistake, confusing him with someone else. Then he felt a sense of growing excitement, a feeling that he had stumbled on something strange and secret. He could not explain it, except that he seemed on the verge of a shattering discovery.

'Here on the night of the storm? Are you sure?'

'It was that night, all right. I'd been out in the woods, see.' He gave a cough and winked knowingly at Phil, then he went on, 'I was hurrying home, the storm was coming up fast. It was in the lane at the back there,' again a jerk of that dirty expressive thumb, 'not this one going down to the road, but the one what cuts across the cottage at the back.'

Phil eyed him narrowly. His second reaction after the excitement engendered by what the man had said at first, was that the person he'd seen must have been none other than the chap from the post-office who'd delivered the telegram on that fatal night. It occurred to him, however, that he would have used the front-gate and left by it, there was no reason for him to use the lane at the back of Lilac Cottage.

'You saw him come from the cottage?' he said.

'Where else?'

This might be important, he thought, what was a strange man doing here in the storm, just about the time of Julie's death? 'Did you see him properly, could you tell what he looked like?'

'I see him in a lightning flash. Who'd bring a big car like that up there, anyway?'

Phil clenched his fists to control his mounting excitement.

'Car? What sort of car?'

'At the end of the lane, just before it turns into the road. Far as I could see it was like one of them big American cars, I couldn't be sure, but I think it was blue. It took up pretty near all the lane, and that's a fact.'

Phil thought desperately. A big American car, with a blue body, whom did he know of who possessed a car like that? He shook his head slowly. There was nobody he could recall.

'This man you saw,' he said, 'what did he look like?'

'I seen him, all right, a feller with a thin face and a moustache. Never saw me, I reckon.'

Phil's brain raced. On the night of the storm, before he had arrived, another man had almost certainly been in the vicinity of the cottage, that seemed certain. Again his thoughts grappled with the mental picture of a large, blue car. Where had he seen a car like that? And a man whose description tallied with that given by the poacher? What would it mean if another man had been at Lilac Cottage round about the time that Julie had died. He glanced at the dark little man, frowning.

'But why didn't you say something about this before?' he said.

'The village copper and me, we don't exactly quarrel,' the man said, 'but I don't go out of my way to get in his way, if you see what I mean. I steers clear of the police and don't get into no trouble.'

'I see.' It was a satisfactory explanation, and Phil was more than ever convinced that the other was telling the truth.

Quite by some miraculous chance he had stumbled on a vital piece of information concerning some stranger lurking round Lilac Cottage, whose existence had never been thought of until this dark stranger had happened to mention it to him now.

'Besides,' the man was saying, his hands deep in his pockets, 'they said it was suicide, didn't they?'

Phil nodded abstractedly. 'That's what they said it was,' he said.

'And I only seen this chap in the flash,' the other went on, 'I couldn't prove anything. What he was doing here, or who he was. All I could say was a blue car, and the chap had a thin white face, and a moustache.'

Phil said nothing. His gaze had turned upon the cottage, there in the gathering dusk, pale and shadows creeping round it. Empty and deserted. He was still trying to think, trying to sort out the implications of this new information that had come from this chance meeting. He was also trying to remember. Surely he had seen a man like that, who answered to the description he had been given, somewhere?

'You couldn't have known that it was anything important,' Phil said.

The man stood watching him while Phil remained silent for some moments. Could it possibly have been Mercury who had come to Lilac

Cottage that night? No, he decided. He did not fit the description. Besides hadn't Thelma said quite definitely that Mercury had been in the Club at the time. Who else, then? For a flash of a second a thought poised like a dagger over his mind. Had Thelma been lying? Had she some reason for saying Mercury was at the Black Moth, when all the time he wasn't? All the time he was somewhere else. At Lilac Cottage with Julie. He dismissed the idea with a feeling of horror against himself for having harboured it.

His mind seized upon Ray Mercury and with vivid clarity recalled the scene outside the Coroner's court at Hatford. A big blue American car, flashy, large as a tank. It had been there, he'd seen it as he left the building. He'd seen Mercury himself, cool and soft-featured and — he gave an involuntary hiss of indrawn breath — a pale man with a thin black moustache who had leaned back in the driving-seat of the car.

Mercury's driver. A pale-faced man, with a black moustache, just as the poacher had described him.

Phil Stone was filled with a mounting anger and excitement, and the desire for revenge against a man unknown to him as yet, a man who was only a face seen and remembered in a flash of lightning on a night of storm and death.

Chapter Twenty

It was next morning and at about the time when the train from Hatford to Waterloo was pulling into London, Thelma Grayson was in a taxi heading for Harley Street. Phil Stone was on the train and though he had looked casually at a morning paper bought at Hatford, it was not such a late edition as the copy which Thelma clutched in her hand, glancing every now and then at the story in the Stop Press.

'4 a.m. Late News. NEW TURN IN NIGHT CLUB DEATH,' she read. 'Understood Scotland Yard not altogether satisfied with the results of earlier inquiries into death of Black Moth night-club owner Ray Mercury, found shot in his office three nights' ago. As a result of certain information received, further investigations being made into circumstances surrounding tragedy.'

Thelma Grayson paid off her taxi outside Harley Street and gave the bell a prolonged agitated ring. When Miss Frayle opened the door Thelma Grayson stood there facing her gripping her newspaper so tightly it might have been a gun she was holding.

'I must see Dr. Morelle —'

'But —?' Miss Frayle began to say, only to be pushed aside, as the visitor dashed past her. Uttering a series of protests, Miss Frayle hurried after the other, who was heading straight for Dr. Morelle's study. She saw her burst in, and then the door slammed behind her.

When Miss Frayle opened the study door and went in she found Thelma Grayson talking vehemently to Dr. Morelle, who was leaning his tall, spare frame casually against his desk. The young woman was sitting in a chair facing him.

'Dr. Morelle,' Thelma Grayson was saying, as Miss Frayle closed the door behind her quietly and stood there drinking in the scene, and then she broke off. She had caught sight of a newspaper on the writing-desk. 'You know,' she said, 'you've seen it. The police have found out he was murdered after all.'

Miss Frayle had crossed to glance at the Stop Press report which Dr. Morelle had pointed out to her earlier, referring to the new turn in the Black Moth business.

Dr. Morelle had stubbed out his cigarette with a nonchalant air.

'I'm glad you have called,' he said. 'I had mentioned to Miss Frayle that I must ask her to telephone you. There were one or two matters I think you might care to know about.'

'Never mind that,' the other said. 'What have you done?' She threw the newspaper she was carrying on to the desk beside the one already there.

Dr. Morelle took a fresh Le Sphinx from the skull cigarette-box, lit it, and said smoothly, through a puff of smoke: 'If it is on account of that newspaper report that you are in a state bordering near hysteria, you may relax.'

'But the police know it wasn't suicide now. It says so there. And the only person who could have made them change their mind is you. Why? I came to you for help and you said you would help me, but all you've done —' Her voice broke, and then she said bitterly: 'All you've done with all your promises is to give me away.'

Dr. Morelle gave the faintest shrug.

'Inspector Hood has his duties to carry out, the same as the rest of us. Who is to blame him if he forgot to bear your feelings in mind at the time when he authorized that press release?'

She stared at him aghast.

'You mean you told him about me?'

Dr. Morelle nodded, and Miss Frayle gave a tiny gasp. This was something he had not mentioned to her, any more than he had mentioned to her that he intended to speak to Thelma Grayson on the telephone, presumably to inform her of the good news he had for her regarding the death of Ray Mercury.

'As a matter of fact I have,' Dr. Morelle was saying to the white-faced, harassed-looking young woman sitting in the chair. 'Inspector Hood of Scotland Yard expressed a wish to meet you. I said I would see if it could be arranged sometime.'

'Oh, my God.' At that agonized cry Miss Frayle went quickly to her side and put her arm sympathetically round the other's shoulder. At the same time she did her best to throw a glare of protest at Dr. Morelle, who was surveying the touching scene with a sardonic expression.

'Perhaps I should add,' he said, examining the tip of his cigarette, 'that I omitted to mention your name. Doubtless, however, that detail may be remedied at a more appropriate moment.'

He gave her the benefit of his wintry smile as her head came up with a jerk, her eyes wide open, gazing at him in bewilderment.

'I — I don't understand.'

'I fancied I had intimated to you that you would be wiser to leave this entire matter in my hands. I can only reiterate that advice, leave all to me.' He nodded at the newspapers on the writing-desk. 'Ignore anything like that which you may read in the press. I can assure you your own situation is not in any way endangered. On the contrary.' His hooded eyes flickered over Miss Frayle who was regarding him with one of her nonplussed expressions with which he was not entirely unfamiliar. 'Perhaps you would remind me, Miss Frayle,' he said, 'what it was about which I was to telephone Miss Grayson this morning.'

But Miss Frayle's eyes behind her horn-rimmed glasses only widened, while her mouth opened and closed soundlessly: 'You mean about — about —?'

'You could not,' Dr. Morelle said, 'have put it more succinctly.'

'What did you want to tell me?'

Thelma Grayson found her voice at last, and her words were a cue for Miss Frayle to plunge into a torrent of explanation. She outlined what Dr. Morelle had told her the previous afternoon following their visit to Tracy Wright's penthouse high above Park Lane and Hyde Park. When the spate abated, the other was on her feet, disbelief written on her face as she glanced first at Miss Frayle and then at Dr. Morelle.

'He gave me blank cartridges?' she kept saying slowly, to herself.

'That's right,' said Miss Frayle, with a bright nod. 'He thought you might get into trouble, you see. Wasn't it clever of him? So although you fired at that horrible man, you didn't hit him and you couldn't have hurt him. Because you only had blank cartridges in the gun.'

Thelma Grayson was staring unseeingly at Dr. Morelle, her hands clenched.

'I didn't shoot him,' she said slowly. 'I couldn't have shot him.' Her attitude slackened. Her shoulders sagged, and her hands hung limply by her sides and she slumped back into her chair. 'I've been tearing myself to pieces, I've almost gone mad. And all the time it was a silly game.'

And then she began to laugh, wildly. She was laughing hysterically, rocking to and fro, and Miss Frayle, with alarmed glances at Dr. Morelle, clutched her arm, trying to quieten her, but the hysterical laughter went on unabated.

Suddenly Miss Frayle felt herself thrust aside and Dr. Morelle had taken Thelma Grayson's shoulders firmly and began speaking to her, quietly, barely raising his voice.

'Calm yourself,' he said. 'You have been under great stress but all that is over. Calm yourself, and relax. Relax.'

There was a strange, mesmeric quality in his tone, his eyes were bent upon the young woman's face, and Miss Frayle saw her eyes open and meet his. And if Miss Frayle experienced a faint jealousy perhaps at the sight of a beautiful young woman held securely by Dr. Morelle's steel-like, yet tender hands, and whose lovely eyes were being subjected to his deeply penetrating gaze, she quickly pushed the idea out of her consciousness.

The other sagged in his grip, her laughter dying to a gurgle. She began to shake violently, and Dr. Morelle handed her over to Miss Frayle who led her gently to her chair. She sat down, her shoulders hunched. Then she burst into tears, and Miss Frayle watched her pityingly.

With a glance at Dr. Morelle she refrained from trying to comfort the other, letting her finish her outburst of pent-up emotion, now quiet and controlled. 'I know,' she said, 'a cup of coffee. That's what you need. I'll make a nice cup of coffee.'

And Miss Frayle bustled out, returning quickly with a tray of rattling coffee-cups.

A little later and calm and smiling Thelma Grayson stepped into a taxi in Harley Street and was driven back to her flat in Charlotte Street. Her fears were at rest, her confidence in Dr. Morelle fully restored. It seemed to her that at last the nightmare in which she had moved like some automaton since that night of horror at the Black Moth was at an end. Outside the front door of her flat she found a figure that had become quite familiar to her during the last few days.

It was Phil Stone.

Chapter Twenty-One

'Don't you see, Thelma, if this man was down at the cottage that night, it might solve at least one problem?' Phil paced the room of the Charlotte Street flat, while Thelma Grayson watched him tensely.

Her first thought when she had found him waiting for her was that he had seen the Stop Press report which had sent her terror-stricken off to Dr. Morelle. But he had made no mention of it, and she presumed that if he had bought a newspaper on the train-journey it had not contained the account of the new turn in the Ray Mercury case.

She decided not to say anything about it to him, it did not affect him and in any case he was so full of the news which had sent him racing back from Little Tiplow to London.

'I don't quite see what you mean?' she said.

'At the inquest you remember the Coroner hinted that it was a bit of a mystery where Julie got the stuff. It's puzzled us, too. Where could she have got it? If that man was Mercury's stooge there's the answer.' Phil clenched a fist, and she saw the knuckles whiten. 'Even if he only gave her that poison, and with it the news which made her take it, then he deserves all that's coming to him.'

'Phil, don't you think you should tell the police?' She looked worried and apprehensive, she was conscious of the steely glitter in his eyes.

'Even if it could be proved that he was hanging around the cottage at the time,' Phil said, 'there's no proof that he ever went in, that he saw Julie. How could the police act, unless they'd got some really solid facts to go on? There's only suspicion, but I'm prepared to act on suspicion alone,' Phil said grimly. He stopped his pacing and turned to Thelma. 'From the description, do you know him?'

'It's almost certainly a man called Luke Roper,' Thelma said, her eyes thoughtful. 'He was Ray Mercury's right-hand man, bodyguard, always drove his car. It sounds like him, from what you say.'

'Do you know him well? This Luke Roper?'

'No. He didn't show up at the club much.'

'You haven't got any idea where he hangs out?'

Thelma shook her head. 'I don't know.'

'I've got to locate him.'

'There's someone who would be able to help,' Thelma said. 'Aces La Rue, he knows a lot about all those people.'

His face lit up with grim anticipation as she moved to the telephone and dialled. Aces La Rue had given her the telephone number of his Soho place when she had seen him there. And she had telephoned him to give him the news of her interview with Dr. Morelle. She could hear the continuous burr-burr at the other end, and was about to give up, believing that he was not in, when the receiver was lifted and his voice, breathless and wheezy, answered. When she said who it was he explained he had been out shopping. He expressed his delight at hearing it was she.

She came straight to the point.

'I wondered if you knew where Luke Roper lives.'

'Luke Roper?' He sounded startled. 'I'd steer clear of that crook, if I were you.'

'Do you know where I can find him?'

'I don't count him among my friends,' Aces La Rue said simply. Then he said: 'He used to have a place not far from Marble Arch.'

'Can you remember the address?'

'Anderson Street, over a café named Pelotti's. But I'm telling you, my dear —'

'Thanks,' Thelma said and rang off before Aces La Rue could launch into a long sermon warning her to keep away from Luke Roper. She gave the address to Phil.

'I'm going over there right away,' he said.

'I'll come, too,' she said quickly.

'No,' he said. 'You'd better keep out of this.'

'Phil,' she clutched his arm. 'You won't do anything — anything risky.'

He grinned. 'I'll remain cool, calm and collected.'

There was a ring at the front-door bell and Thelma gave a start. Phil thought he caught a glint of apprehension in her eyes. She went to the door and opened it.

'Why, Miss Frayle,' she said. 'Come in.'

Miss Frayle came in, her eyes shining. She was hardly inside the flat, before she began to speak, but Thelma Grayson said quickly. 'Mr. Stone's just going, you've come in time to see him.'

Miss Frayle did not quite take the hint and was about to say what was on the tip of her tongue, until the other gesticulated to her to remain silent.

'What a lovely afternoon it is,' Miss Frayle said promptly, at the top of her voice. She saw Phil Stone who had appeared in the little hall, and smiled at him. She had not seen him since the Black Moth, when he had appeared utterly shocked and stricken. She thought he still looked somewhat ill and anxious now. Taut and edgy, she thought, as if he was about to take a vital step. She knew from what Thelma Grayson had told Dr. Morelle that the two knew each other.

'I'm just on my way, Miss Frayle,' Phil Stone said.

'I'm sorry, Mr. Stone,' Miss Frayle said automatically, but her expression was not markedly depressed. She in fact was longing for him to leave, so that she could talk to Thelma Grayson.

'How is your Dr. Morelle?' the young man was asking her politely.

'My Dr. Morelle?' Miss Frayle said with a nervous giggle. 'He's not mine, he belongs to no one but himself, I do assure you.' She was going to add something to the effect that she wished he did belong to her, that he was hers, but decided not to, and blushed instead. 'He's very well, thank you,' she said.

'Please remember me to him,' Phil Stone said politely, and Miss Frayle promised to do so. She caught a glance between him and the young woman she'd come to see, and then he was gone.

Chapter Twenty-Two

Phil Stone picked up a taxi in Charlotte Street and drove to Marble Arch, alighting on the corner of a street behind the Odeon Cinema, to look for Anderson Street. Now that the rising excitement generated by his talk with Thelma Grayson was over, he felt cool and calm. Only the hard gleam in his eyes hinted at the cold hatred in his heart for the man he sought, and he knew that if it came to a showdown all his pent-up bitter fury would burst out in a blaze of violence.

Anderson Street was a small street dominated by a large block of flats on one side. On the other side of the street stucco-fronted, vari-coloured houses given over to apartments, and flats. There were several shops and a couple of pubs. Phil found Pelotti's, a rather grubby-looking restaurant, which was filling up with lunch-time clients. The door at the side of the restaurant was open, and Phil went into the short hall, and straight up the stairs. They were creaking and uncarpeted, and the smell of cooking from the restaurant rose up with him in his nostrils.

On the second floor he saw a door at the end of a dim landing, and he went along to it and rang the bell. There was silence within, though he thought he heard soft music as if a radio was on, but turned low. Then he heard soft footsteps. The door opened, and he looked into the dead bits of slate that were the eyes of the man he had last seen in the big American blue car outside Hatford Coroner's Court. This was the man that the poacher had seen hanging about Lilac Cottage on the night Julie had died. This was Luke Roper, the late Ray Mercury's stooge and hired thug.

'Well?'

The voice was sibilant and cold, toneless and without life, like the eyes in his pale expressionless face.

'Luke Roper?'

'What's it to you?'

'I want to talk to you,' Phil said and he moved forward.

Something flickered in the other's eyes. The teeth beneath the thin strip of moustache were bared for a moment, as it seemed he would shut the door, but Phil kept moving forward and his hefty shoulder pushed the door further open.

'Okay,' Luke Roper said, as he stood beside Phil in the sitting room of the flat. 'If you got anything to say, get it over and beat it.'

Phil gave a look round the room, which was furnished very ordinarily, in contrast to the flashily-dressed individual before him. Some darkish wall-paper covered the walls, there were a couple of arm-chairs and a divan, and there was a bureau with the flap open in one corner. He had the impression that the other had rented the flat furnished. He gave his attention to Luke Roper.

'You knew Julie Grayson, didn't you?' he said.

'Of course I knew her,' Luke said. 'She was always hanging round Ray Mercury, at the Black Moth, and I used to be around there myself sometimes.'

Phil looked at him, his jaw set, his eyes narrowed. There came the strident hoot of a taxi in the street below above the rumble of the traffic milling round Marble Arch.

'You knew her better than that,' he said. 'You were at the cottage at Little Tiplow the night she died.'

Luke Roper made no reply, his expression seemed to remain unchanged. Or did it seem to freeze with malevolence and menace? His eyes in the pale face were as dead as they had been before. And then Phil caught a twitch in the hands the other held at his side. He smiled grimly to himself.

'You were seen,' he said. 'You didn't know that did you?'

'Nobody could have seen me,' Luke Roper said, 'because I wasn't there.'

Phil grinned at him. 'You drove away in Ray Mercury's car, just before the storm broke. After you'd left Julie Grayson. I can produce a witness to prove it, to point you out to the police.'

The other shrugged slightly, still standing there motionless, reminding Phil of some reptile, poised preparatory to striking. He said nothing.

'You gave her the poison which killed her,' Phil said, and now a cold fury took possession him. Suddenly some instinct cried out to him that this creature had been directly responsible for the death of the girl he loved.

He was not prepared for Luke Roper's reaction to his words. Stark hatred glared from the pallid face, life flickered in the eyes, the thin moustache was drawn back in a snarl, and his hand shot inside his jacket. In the same moment the hand reappeared and Phil heard the snick of an opening knife-blade.

'You better be on your way, before I cut you to ribbons.'

It was the sight of the knife that did it. With a growl of anger Phil dived, moving fast, and before Luke could slash at him with the knife, he had grabbed the other's wrist, twisting viciously. Luke fought to throw him off. But Phil twisted the man's arm behind his back and pressed up relentlessly as the man squirmed. He acted so swiftly that Luke Roper had been caught off his guard. Phil heard him gasp with agony.

Luke Roper found it impossible to hold the knife, it dropped from his paralysed fingers, and in that instant Phil hit him, his fist crashing against his jaw and hurling him back against the divan.

Phil went after him, giving him no quarter, battering him with punches in a primitive fury. He found Luke stronger than he looked, he was tough and steely. He fought back, clawing at Phil's hair, his thumbs trying to gouge his eyes, and as they grappled in a fierce clinch they rolled to the floor.

Phil fell underneath his opponent, and at first he thought the other meant to reach for his knife, which lay where it had fallen, a few feet way. Then he saw the deadly intent in the man's glittering eyes as, blood trickling from the side of his mouth, he hooked his finger's swiftly round Phil's throat and began to squeeze.

Phil brought his knee up sharply. With a groan of agony Luke relaxed his vicious grip and Phil struck him again, jerking his head back sickeningly. He caught him another tremendous blow over his ear and Luke fell to one side. Phil scrambled to his feet, hauling him up and hit him again. Arms flailing wildly, Luke crashed backwards, to be brought up against the bureau, overturning it in a litter of papers.

Blood was streaming from the gash which he had opened under his eye, Luke came up blindly at Phil, who sent him reeling round the room, with a series of blows and there was grim and bitter satisfaction in every punch he threw. Finally, Luke Roper staggered against a table, which went over with a crash, and a chair splintered as Luke collapsed on it, completely unconscious. Phil bent over him, gulping for air, and it was then that he saw something gleaming amongst the wreckage. It had rolled from the direction of the bureau, and he picked it up. It was a small capsule, and as he stood, regaining his breath, the sight of it struck a chord at the back of his mind.

He dropped the capsule into his pocket, though he didn't quite know the reason for doing so, and then with a look of satisfaction at the figure sprawled amongst the wreckage of the room, he went out, slamming the door behind him, and down the stairs.

As he reached the door to the street, Thelma Grayson, accompanied by Miss Frayle, appeared, hurrying into the entrance. They saw him and instinctively Phil straightened his tie and tried to smooth his hair.

'Are you all right?' Thelma said.

He nodded. 'Enjoyed every minute of it,' he said. 'Knocked the living daylights out of him.'

Miss Frayle's eyes were round behind her horn-rims. 'We were afraid you might run into some trouble,' she said.

'Luke's the one who ran into trouble,' Phil said.

Thelma Grayson had taken his arm and was urging him towards the street. 'Come away quickly,' she said, with a look upstairs, 'we've got a taxi.'

He wiped a smear of blood from his chin. 'I've nothing to hang around for here,' he said. 'I've done what I came to do.' And he allowed himself to be hurried out to the taxi. As they drove off a sudden flash of revelation struck him and he dipped his fingers into his pocket. He brought out the capsule and showed it to Thelma. He was recalling now why it had at once attracted his attention. And the significance of its presence in the wrecked room he had just quitted dawned upon him in all its force.

'Remember the inquest?' he said. 'They said the poison Julie took might have been in something like this.'

She looked at the gleaming object in his hand. Miss Frayle took it gingerly for a moment to look at it, then handed it back.

'I found it at that rat's place,' Phil said.

'It's the sort of thing Dr. Morelle would like to have a look at,' Miss Frayle said. And Phil Stone's head came up with a jerk at her words.

'Let's take it to him,' he said. 'Now.'

Chapter Twenty-Three

Dr. Morelle was toying delicately with the capsule Phil Stone had handed him, in his study in Harley Street. Thelma Grayson, Phil Stone and Miss Frayle watched him, each with an air of suppressed excitement.

It was early afternoon, Dr. Morelle had just come in after a lunch-appointment, to find Miss Frayle and the other two awaiting him. The three of them had grabbed sandwiches and coffee on their way back from Anderson Street.

It had been an afterthought of Dr. Morelle's which had prompted him to send Miss Frayle along to the Charlotte Street flat with instructions to impress upon Thelma Grayson that there was no necessity ever to describe to any other living soul the part she had played in the macabre business at the Black Moth. It was to be a secret locked in the hearts of the three of them, Thelma Grayson, Dr. Morelle and Miss Frayle, which would help no one if it were told.

'Tell her she'd make me an accessory after the fact,' Dr. Morelle had said to Miss Frayle with a sardonic smile. 'And if she goes about telling people she'll get me into trouble with the police. Simply because she was innocent all the time doesn't alter my position, which was to have placed the knowledge in my possession in the hands of Scotland Yard.'

Miss Frayle had carried out her errand after Phil Stone had left to call upon Luke Roper, and Thelma Grayson had agreed to take Dr. Morelle's advice very much to heart. Then she had accompanied her in the taxi to Anderson Street.

'You say you chanced upon this in the man's flat?' Dr. Morelle said, turning to Phil Stone.

'After the fight. It had rolled out of a drawer in the bureau that got knocked over.' Dr. Morelle glanced at the graze on the other's jaw and his eyes twinkled. 'Miss Frayle suggested that you might be interested in having a look at it.'

'Miss Frayle was right,' Dr. Morelle said, and Miss Frayle blushed suitably. It was not often that Dr. Morelle unburdened himself to the extent of paying her a compliment.

'You'd better come with me,' Dr. Morelle said to the three of them.

They followed him out of the study, across the hall into his laboratory. Miss Frayle closed the door behind her and with the two others bent her attention upon Dr. Morelle. He made his way to a bench, where he concentrated himself fully upon his task.

The laboratory was small, but had been constructed under Dr. Morelle's supervision, so that every inch was utilized to the full. All around was the most modern equipment in gleaming steel and glass occupying the shelves, cupboards and benches. In one corner taps shone over a bright sink. There were stacks of basins of varying sizes, in copper, aluminium and porcelain. Beakers, graduated flasks, specimen-jars, miscellaneous pipettes stood in orderly array.

A wonderful and complicated apparatus for micro-analysis, with improvements designed by Dr. Morelle himself, took up the entire length of one bench. Mortars and pestles, retorts and bulbs, crucibles and test-glasses winked and glinted from the shelves. Racks of test-tubes, syphons, funnels and condensers filled the glass-fronted cupboards.

On one wall a synchronous clock silently registered the passing seconds. An electric signal timing clock stood near an analytical precision balance, capable of accurately weighing the minutest portion of a single hair. There was a percentage hygrometer, and a thermograph, towards which Miss Frayle inevitably turned to watch, fascinated, the delicate tracing of the pen.

Soon Dr. Morelle turned from the bench to bring the small test-tube he carried over to Phil Stone and Thelma Grayson, Miss Frayle hovering in the background.

The two others could smell the aroma of bitter almonds emanating from the test-tube.

'It's the same smell that was round Julie's mouth,' Phil said.

Dr. Morelle nodded. 'That capsule contained a lethal dose of cyanide.' He turned towards Thelma Grayson. 'It is suggested,' he said, 'that this is the form in which your sister took the poison which killed her.' He looked at the test-tube with a faint frown, as if expressing his feeling of revulsion towards whoever was responsible for putting the deadly poison in the dead girl's possession.

'Am I not right in saying that at the inquest the view was expressed that the poison might have been administered in some such capsule?' he said.

Thelma nodded her head slightly.

'That is correct,' Phil said quietly.

'When you first found her, was there anything particularly that struck you about her appearance? Anything which suggests to you, on reflection, a method by which she took the poison?'

'She was tensed, with an expression of great pain and horror,' Phil spoke in a low voice.

'Anything else?'

Phil hesitated. 'I did notice something about her mouth. They referred to it at the inquest, I remember. She might have pinched her nose and mouth, to —'

He broke off, with a glance at Thelma.

Dr. Morelle appeared lost in thought. 'The poison administered in a capsule,' he said, half to himself, 'such as was found at the flat of this man Luke Roper, an associate of the late Ray Mercury.'

Phil Stone had informed Dr. Morelle of his visit to Little Tiplow, his shattering discovery through his meeting with the poacher that Luke Roper had been seen at Lilac Cottage on the fatal night, and his determination to have it out with Ray Mercury's one-time right-hand man. He had gone on to describe his visit to the flat over Pelotti's shop.

'What exactly did you say to this man?' Dr. Morelle was asking him now.

'I accused him of being at the cottage on the night of Julie's death. I bluffed a little, I told him he'd given her the poison. I must have caught him completely unawares, because he never tried to call my bluff. I knew he knew a hell of a lot about what had happened, and he knew I knew it. It was that really started things going.'

'You felt that your accusation really had struck home?'

Phil Stone nodded. 'It was that started the row.'

Dr. Morelle said musingly: 'It struck near the truth, and he was very much alarmed.' He eyed the other with interest. 'This information you have given me opens up a new avenue of approach to the case.'

'What does it suggest to you?' Thelma Grayson said.

'There is no proof. There are no witnesses.' His voice trailed off musingly. Suddenly he seemed to rouse himself out of these deep ruminations, and spoke directly to Phil Stone, 'are you prepared to put yourself in my hands?'

The other stared at him, wonderingly. 'Yes,' he said, 'of course.'

'Go from here back to Baker Street, and keep your eyes open, be very careful and watchful of strangers. Don't try to be clever and tangle Luke Roper any more. You've done more than enough, playing a lone hand. Next time you might not be so fortunate.'

There was a grave note in Dr. Morelle's voice and Phil Stone solemnly assured him he would keep out of the way of any potential danger.

'I have a plan of my own for Luke Roper,' Dr. Morelle said. 'And I don't want pugilistic young men like you interfering, to spoil it.'

The three of them began asking him questions, but he retained an enigmatic composure, and presently Phil Stone and Thelma Grayson went off together, their curiosity unsatisfied.

After they had gone, Miss Frayle, unable to stem her inquisitiveness, said to Dr. Morelle: 'I don't understand what all that was about.'

He smiled at her bleakly. 'There are moments, my dear Miss Frayle,' he said, 'when faith is more desirable than understanding. I believe I can turn this situation to good account. I am convinced that there is a solution to this whole affair, which lacking proof as I do at the moment, I should find difficult to reach in any manner other than the one I now propose to adopt.'

He started to pace the study, his firmly carved chin sunk on his chest, while Miss Frayle threw herself into a chair.

'A trap must be set,' Dr. Morelle said presently.

'A trap?' Miss Frayle said. 'For whom?'

'For Ray Mercury's murderer,' Dr. Morelle said.

Miss Frayle uttered a gasp, but Dr. Morelle gave her no respite. 'I wish you to type a note, Miss Frayle,' he said.

She jumped up and grabbed her notebook and pencil. 'Who to?'

'You will not require your notebook,' Dr. Morelle said. 'It will be brief and you can type it straight down. Please use plain paper.'

Miss Frayle regarded him with some surprise and moved to her desk before the typewriter. She placed some paper into the machine and sat there poised expectantly. Dr. Morelle pondered for a few moments, and then said:

'Type this, Miss Frayle. 'I know something about Ray Mercury's death the police do not know, but would like to. Meet me at the Black Moth to-night at nine o'clock sharp, or it will be the worse for you.''

Miss Frayle's eyebrows rose, and her glasses slipped down her nose as she rattled the message off. She looked up, her expression completely baffled and Dr. Morelle smiled at her thinly.

'Sign it 'X',' he said suavely. 'That would seem to be an appropriately compelling pseudonym.'

'But who's it to?'

Dr. Morelle made no answer, instead he picked up the telephone and dialled Scotland Yard. As he waited to be put through to Inspector Hood, a thought occurred to him and he spoke to Miss Frayle:

'If you could whip up your flagging energy sufficiently,' he said, 'to type out precisely the same message on a separate piece of paper, I should be greatly obliged to you.'

Miss Frayle glared at him and would no doubt have uttered some words of protest, except for the fact that Dr. Morelle would not have been listening to her.

He was speaking incisively into the telephone to Inspector Hood.

Chapter Twenty-Four

The figure paused on the corner of Meard Street, and went a few yards along Frith Street before turning into another street, narrow and ill-lit, where the once familiar neon sign jutting out above the pavement was now dark. No longer was the shape of a black moth picked out in crimson neon, no more did its eyes flash on and off underneath the name: The Black Moth.

No cars or taxis were driving up to set down visitors to the club, no stalwart, saluting figure of the commissionaire in his opulent-looking uniform. Quickly the figure passed the club shuttered and dark, until it reached the alley, black and cavernous beyond which it knew lay the yard, upon which opened the back entrance to the Black Moth.

The figure went quickly down the alley and into the darkness of the yard.

There were no lights in the yard, but the shadow moved unerringly to the iron staircase that led to the door of the passage, which in turn led to the late Ray Mercury's private office at the back of the club. The figure went up the iron stairs, the soft scuffing of its shoes was the only sound as it reached the door.

Glancing over its shoulder into the darkness the figure slipped the key into the lock with infinite care and quiet. A moment, and the shadowy shape was inside, with the door closed behind it, standing listening in the silence and darkness.

The figure brushed against a door, paused to listen, hesitated as if it was about to turn back to explore the main part of the premises, when it saw the thin wedge of light from the door of Ray Mercury's office.

The shape stole forward and kicked the door open suddenly.

Even Luke Roper's self-control deserted him for a moment, as he stood there in the doorway eyeing the woman whose pale blonde hair shimmered in the light as she leaned casually against the ornately-carved writing-desk.

Greta Mercury herself was equally astonished by Luke Roper's sudden appearance. Then her strangely green slanting eyes turned to cold anger.

'So it was you?' she said in a harsh voice.

Luke Roper recovered his composure swiftly. He prided himself on his coolness and self-control, and despite the shock he had received, this was a time for wariness. Something had gone wrong. He couldn't believe it was Ray Mercury's widow who had sent him that mysterious note inviting him to be at the Black Moth to-night.

'What are you talking about?' he said. He fingered the painful bruise which ran along his jaw-bone. 'What was me?'

'You sent me that note saying you knew something about Ray's death. I was to be here to-night. Or else, you said. Do you mean to try to blackmail me?'

So she'd had a similar mysterious invitation, too? But Luke allowed none of his surprise to show in his face. He shrugged, watching her.

'You're talking like you're crazy,' he said softly. 'Anyway what is there to put the black on you about?'

'You're on to something, you rat,' she said.

'Guilty conscience, eh? I'll tell you something. Since we've met up this way, and I feel chatty, I'll tell you. I never believed he shot himself, if that's what's worrying you. Too fond of life, and of girls —'

The ice-green eyes flashed and her face contorted.

'Hit you on the raw, eh?' Luke Roper said with a chuckle. 'I had a few ideas who might have given him lead-poisoning, but why should I tell? I never mentioned to no one how there was a certain party who knew Ray's handwriting better than anybody. I wonder what the cops would have done if somebody had tipped them off it was that certain someone who might have written that note so no one could have told the diff?'

'You think I did it?'

'You had as good a motive as anyone. You were crazy jealous of him.' His thin moustache curled back over his teeth. 'But I don't have to think anymore, now. Now I know for sure you did it. You just gave yourself away.'

'If it wasn't you who sent the note,' she said, 'why have you turned up?'

'I happened to be passing,' he said, he didn't see why he should tell a thing more than he needed to her. 'Thought I'd drop in, just for old times' sake. I'm glad I did. I learnt something. Now I know you killed Ray, it might be worth something to me, if I needed it.'

'All right, I shot him,' she said, her tone emotionless. 'You won't make anything out of it. I gave him all the chances but he just laughed at me. I'd made up my mind already after I'd seen him here that night, when he had the nerve to say he couldn't help it.'

'I know,' he said, interrupting her. 'I saw you come out, remember? Sometime before he was found.'

'I returned the back way after I'd left the front way. I found him recovering from a shock. He was deathly white. Perhaps somebody had come in and told him what he really was. I don't know. But I walked up to him and he didn't move, just stared at me, thinking I was going to plead with him, I suppose. I shot him from close up. I was wearing my evening gloves, and I put the gun in his hand and wrote that note. I went out the way I came, and nobody was any the wiser.'

'Why are you telling me all this?'

'Why? I could kill you, too, like stamping on a spider.'

Luke moved only slightly, but there was a metallic snick and the knife gleamed in his hand.

'You could kill me?' he said silkily. 'Not so easily as you killed him.'

She was staring at him, her slanting eyes narrowed green slits.

'I'd carve you to ribbons,' he said. 'Or maybe you'd like it the way the girl did? The Grayson kid. A nice little cyanide pill, as prescribed by your late hubby?'

She started as if he had struck her across her beautiful mask-like face.

'You did — that?'

Luke laughed. 'He didn't like to do the dirty work,' he said. 'And she'd got to know too much. She was always hanging around him, and somehow, we never knew how, she caught on about the dope-racket. Or maybe you didn't know about that side of the business?'

'I knew,' she said, and her tone was tinged with weariness.

'I'd have killed her then,' he said. 'But he thought he could talk her out of it. She was sweet on him, you see. But it opened her eyes, that little discovery. He didn't know which way she'd jump, and he got frightened. Shake her off and silence her with one move, that was his idea. And I had to do it.'

He paused as if waiting for her to speak. But she didn't say anything. Something about her expression, her attitude started a thin snake of fear crawling down his spine. He started talking again.

'So now we know something about each other,' he said. 'I fixed her and made it look like she'd fixed herself, you killed him and they tagged it the same way. We should be partners, we're so smart.'

His quiet laugh died on his lips as the gun suddenly appeared in her hand. It was a black Smith and Wesson .38. A man-stopper all right, and her finger was squeezing on the trigger.

'That's right,' she was saying. 'That girl; then Ray; and now it's your turn.'

Dr. Morelle, Inspector Hood and Miss Frayle, together with two plainclothes men, who were crouched amongst the dusty furniture in the next-door room, tensed.

Through the microphone hidden under Ray Mercury's desk, every word between his widow and Luke Roper had been coming over the headphones worn by Hood and Dr. Morelle, at the same time it was also being recorded as damning evidence on the spinning spools of the portable tape-recording machine which was being operated by one of the plainclothes men.

Miss Frayle, taut and quivering with excitement, beside Dr. Morelle, could hear the words only faintly through his ear-phones.

'What are they saying?' she was whispering excitedly. 'I can't hear.'

Dr. Morelle silenced her with a glowering look.

'She's pulled a gun,' Inspector Hood said hoarsely, as Dr. Morelle was already leaping to the door, his head-phones flung off.

'Come on,' he rapped.

But even as Dr. Morelle, followed by Hood and the two plainclothes detectives raced out into the passage towards the office, Miss Frayle heard the crashing report of the shot over the discarded earphones. She was running herself now, after Dr. Morelle and Inspector Hood.

Dr. Morelle and the others burst into the office to find Luke Roper lying sprawled, his gaze turned sightlessly at the ceiling, a bullet-hole in his forehead. Greta Mercury leaned against the desk, smoke wisping from the muzzle of her pocket revolver.

'Drop that,' Inspector Hood barked, lunging forward. The blonde woman jerked to life, like some marionette. Her lips drew back from her teeth as, mouthing some incoherent words, she raised the gun.

Hood closed with her, wrenching the revolver from her hand. She fought furiously, her nails clawing down his face, and tore herself free. Before Dr. Morelle, or the other two detectives, impeded by the staggering inspector could reach her, she had twisted her way out of the office. She flung open the door at the end of the passage, stood framed for a fraction of a second against the darkness of the yard beyond, and then her heels went clacking down the iron stairs.

Inspector Hood and the detective charged after her. But Dr. Morelle, shrugging, stood aside and indicated to Miss Frayle who was about to rush after the others, to remain where she was.

'It is now a matter for the police,' he said.

Miss Frayle adjusted her spectacles which inevitably had slipped half-way down her nose.

Inspector Hood and the detectives had run out of the alley into the street beside the Black Moth in time to hear the roar of a car-engine. It raced away furiously, swinging recklessly out into Frith Street.

As the police-officers ran towards the dark, gleaming police-car parked inconspicuously on the other side of Frith Street, Greta Mercury hurled her car furiously round a corner. Inspector Hood and the others in the police-car gave chase. Taxis and cars pulled aside, staring pedestrians showed them the direction the fugitive had wildly taken.

There came a distant crash, the rending of metal and the tinkling of glass. The swiftly-milling crowd parted as the police-car reached the lights of Cambridge Circus. Hurtling round the curve, Greta Mercury's car had mounted the pavement, struck a corner of the Palace Theatre and turned completely over.

Greta Mercury was behind the wheel, slumped like a rag-doll. Her neck was broken.

Back at the Black Moth, a young uniformed policeman had appeared on the scene, and Dr. Morelle, leaving him in charge of Luke Roper's body and the tape-recording machine made his way, accompanied by Miss Frayle, down the iron staircase into the yard. Dr. Morelle's pencil electric-torch illuminated their path and Miss Frayle clutched on to his arm, they went through the alley into the street.

Miss Frayle still hung on to Dr. Morelle as they reached the street corner, and they turned back to look at the darkened sign of the Black Moth. Dr. Morelle had given the policeman who had remained behind a message for Inspector Hood to the effect that since there was nothing more for him that he could usefully do at the club he was returning to Harley Street.

'Here's a taxi,' Miss Frayle said, as a taxi with its disengaged sign shining out against the darkness of the street appeared. 'Let's get back and I'll make a nice cup of tea.'

But Dr. Morelle did not raise his sword-stick to hail the oncoming taxi. Instead he turned to her with a sardonic expression. 'We will walk, Miss

Frayle; there is nothing more conducive to thirst for a cup of tea than a stroll through London at night.'

Miss Frayle sighed, what with one thing and another it had been a pretty trying day. She was about to suggest that although he, being the human dynamo he was, might not be feeling the effects of the long, tiring day, she was only human after all, when she realized he had already made off with his long, raking stride, and she stood alone on the shadowy street corner. A man's olive-skinned face stared boldly into hers, and with a stifled cry, Miss Frayle shot forward at a run and caught up with Dr. Morelle's tall figure.

He did not turn as she breathlessly half-trotted alongside him. In an effort to slow his pace to hers she slipped her arm through his once more. But he did not notice her even then, nor did he slacken his speed perceptibly. She looked up at the lean saturnine features and sighed to herself. His thoughts were obviously miles away, no doubt ruminating on the strange case which had reached its dramatic climax only a little while ago.

Together, Dr. Morelle, his sword-stick rapping on the pavement and Miss Frayle, made their way through Soho towards Harley Street.

If you enjoyed *Callers for Dr. Morelle*, please share your thoughts on Amazon by leaving a review.

For more free and discounted eBooks every week, sign up to our Endeavour Media newsletter.

Follow us on Twitter and Instagram.